POOR ANGUS

Robin Jenkins

CANONGATE

First published in Great Britain in 2000
by Canongate Books Ltd,
14 High Street, Edinburgh EH1 1TE

10 9 8 7 6 5 4 3 2 1

Copyright © Robin Jenkins 2000

The moral rights of the author have been asserted

British Library Cataloguing-in-Publication Data
A catalogue record for this book is
available on request from the British Library

ISBN 1 84195 002 5

www.canongate.net
Typeset by Hewer Text
Printed and bound by
Creative Print and Design (Wales), Ebbw Vale

In memory of Colin

'In my own country where I most desire'
Milton

PART ONE

PART ONE

1

The island was a painter's paradise, except for one thing: the absence of amenable women.

The light had such freshness and clarity that he could not help having sympathy with those, well represented among the islanders, who believed in the Biblical account of creation. There were dawns when, at the door of his house, on the sea-loch's edge, he cried out in wonder and joy. It seemed as if the blue inlets, the pale pink sands, the green rocky hills, and in the distance the mauve mountains of neighbouring islands, all ideas forming in the Great Painter's mind for millennia, had during the past five minutes been executed, and here they were now complete and perfect to the tiniest shell and minuscule flower, with the celestial paint not yet dry. He had once gone bounding bare as Adam along the sands, trying to express his gratitude and delight. Luckily it was a remote shore, with none of those rather less successful creatures, people, to observe and misinterpret his corybantic gallop.

There were other mornings, to be truthful rather more numerous, when sheets of rain obscured everything, but he knew that next day, or the next, or the one after that, for closeness to the Atlantic provided procession upon procession of heavy clouds, all would be revealed again, fresher than ever.

He had painted scenes more exotic than these, in a far-off part of the world, but here the bright green grass and the rocks made smooth by tide and wind, were kin to his own flesh and bones, for he too had been created on this island, 43 years ago.

Whenever he painted it, whether the myriads of flowers on the machair or the puffins on the sea cliffs or the Celtic crosses in the abandoned graveyards, he was trying to convey his love and loyalty, as well as the the longings of his soul. It was a pity, therefore, though hardly a surprise, that his fellow islanders dismissed his work as gaudy smudges and him as an eccentric fraud.

He had been born in Kildonan, the island's capital and only town. After his mother's death, when he was ten, he had been taken to Glasgow by his father, a post-office official. In time he had graduated from the Glasgow School of Art, and at the age of 24 had obtained a post as Lecturer in Art at a Teachers' Training College in Basah, then a British colony between the South China Sea and the Sea of Sulu. There he had taught, travelled, painted, and made love for 17 years until, with the advent of *Merdeka*, or Independence, certain changes, such as the substitution of Malay for English as the language of instruction and the promotion over him of his Malay assistant, had caused him to accept a substantial sum in return for the cancelling of his contract. This, added to money he had saved, had enabled him two years ago to retire to Flodday and plan master-pieces, as he had long dreamed of doing. On one of his leaves he had bought a disused school with house attached at Ardnave Point, the remotest promontory. Its water supply was a spring that dried up in a prolonged drought and it had no telephone or electricity, but the isolation and beauty of its position more than compensated.

On the strength of three paintings on display in a Glasgow gallery, he had already established the beginnings of a reputation. He had been mentioned in a *Herald* review as an interesting new painter. The boldness of his colours, 'the influence of the tropics' particularly in his portraits of women, had been noticed,

He liked painting female nudes and had done so often in Basah, using Chinese, Malay, Filipina, and Australian women as models, but he had found Flodday women too prudish, owing to

4

the influence of the Free Kirk, and the few he had approached had rebuffed him. One indeed had reported him to the police. On the other hand, an importunate holiday-maker from Edinburgh had had to be repulsed, not because she was uncomely, for that did not matter to a painter seeking truth, but because she had made it too obvious that it was not only his brush she was eager to oblige. He had painted with enthusiasm women whose adiposity would have scunnered ordinary men, but he had slept only with those he thought beautiful. He had high standards too, having made love with the most delectable of women, Fidelia Gomez, descended from Portuguese explorers and Filipino headhunters. Dark-skinned and voluptuous, she was in his bedroom at Ardnave, in one of his most triumphant paintings.

Just when he was having to admit that the loneliness wasn't as fruitful as he had hoped, he met Janet.

He came into the lounge bar of the Kildonan Hotel about five o'clock one sunny Saturday in June, and there she was behind the bar. She probably noticed him first, for with his greying beard, white hat, green corduroy suit, and open-toed sandals, he was conspicuous. Also he had a way of entering such places with snorts and with his head held high, like a lion visiting a watering-hole that inferior creatures also frequented. If his worth as a painter had been recognised, as it ought, he would have been humble. Until then he needed some self-protective arrogance.

He was the only customer. He stood at the bar and ordered a whisky and lemonade, a mixture considered a desecration by local men, many of whom worked in distilleries that produced famous malts.

It was only then that he really noticed the new barmaid. If ever he wanted to paint Deirdre of the Sorrows, this tall, pale, raven-haired young woman would make the perfect model. High cheekbones gave her blue eyes a tragic keenness, as if she had been the cause of bloody jealousies among the caterans. She was wearing black slacks and a sleeveless red blouse that gave a

5

glimpse of a small but assertive bosom. No rings adorned her fingers but she wore jade earrings of Celtic design, and on her blouse, at the cleft between her breasts, was a brooch in the shape of an eagle with outspread wings.

Under her right eye was a bluish mark. It could have been the remains of a bruise, or veins showing through her delicate skin.

She was staring at him with what in another woman would have been flattering interest. In her it looked more like impudence.

'You'll be the painter then,' she said.

There were several painters on the island. Some of their work hung on the walls, for sale at immodest prices: straightforward, anaemic representations of island scenes. But yes, he was *the* painter. So he nodded.

She did not seem to be competent or conscientious at her job. Perhaps, being a Celtic princess, she considered serving menials beneath her dignity. He smiled at his own little joke. But if he did not want his drink flung in his face he had better not be seen laughing at her. There was menace in the jingle of her earrings.

'You're new here,' he said.

'Started on Wednesday.'

'From an island, further north?'

'Skye originally. Glasgow, recently.'

Skye, where the mountains were high and fierce. Glasgow, where the women were frank and not easily abashed.

'I hear you live at the back of beyond,' she said.

A strange remark from a native of Skye where there were many backs of beyond.

He wondered why, so newly arrived, she had been finding out about him.

'You're just back from the Far East,' she said.

'Two years ago.'

'Whereabouts were you?'

'Basah.'

6

'Where's that?'

'About a thousand miles east of Singapore.'

'Is that in the tropics?'

'Yes.'

'How long were you there?'

'Seventeen years.'

'You must have liked it if you stayed all that time.'

'I liked it very much.'

'What were you doing there?'

'I lectured on Art in a Teachers' Training College.'

Suddenly memories of Fidelia flooded his mind; of her walking so elegantly, in sarong and *kebaya*, in the grounds of the College; of her pleading on behalf of some unfortunate student whom other members of the staff, himself included, wished to expel. Everyone had liked and admired her. Many had tolerated him for her sake. They had thought that he must have qualities they themselves could not see in him, otherwise so intelligent, so beautiful, and so honest a woman as Fidelia Gomez would never have loved him.

'I was going to ask if you had a woman there,' said the barmaid, 'but I don't have to. You see, I have second sight.' She closed her eyes. 'She's still in your mind, isn't she? Tall. Dark. Thick lips. Jet-black hair. Tight skirt down to her ankles.'

It would have described a thousand women in Basah.

'Why didn't you bring her back with you?'

If he had said, 'She wouldn't come', it would have been true and yet it would have been a lie. He had not wanted her to come.

At the airport, holding her hand, he had told her, with tears in his eyes, that if ever she needed a refuge she was to come to him, but both of them had known they would never see each other again. She had written three letters. He had not answered them. There had seemed no point in their torturing themselves with protestations of love when they were 10,000 miles apart. Besides

7

there was Gomez, her husband, threatening to reclaim her at any time; and there was little Letty.

'That's an unusual shirt,' said the barmaid. 'What's it made of?'

'Pineapple fibre. From the Philippines.'

Where Fidelia had come from too, and where Gomez still lived. He was a Manila racketeer.

'I'm told your cottage is full of Satanic objects.'

Locals came and peeped in the windows. Once they had nailed a sheep's skull to the door. It was still there. It wasn't often that vandals made improvements.

'I'd like to see them.'

He had never trusted women who invited themselves.

'How about tomorrow?' she asked. 'When they're all in church.'

Before he could tell her 'Nothing doing', the bar was besieged by a horde of local young men and women. He had to take his drink and his hat over to a corner.

He was soon joined by three long-haired youths, named respectively, as he soon learned, Donald, Dugald, and Torry, abbreviated no doubt from Torquil. They had pint glasses of lager in their hands and at first paid him no heed, being too fascinated by the new barmaid. Their admiration of her, though lustful enough, was restrained. Something about her intimidated them. Perhaps at 30 or so she was too old for them, or they recognised in her some sinister quality, like second sight.

Eventually they turned to, or rather on, Angus. Their sort had baited him before. They were under the delusion that he lacked virility. Nell Ballantyne would have put them right, with Australian forthrightness and profanity. He hoped Nell was reconciled with her big, beer-bellied, philandering, golf maniac. Angus had assured her, too, that if she was ever in trouble she should come to him: he would look after her. Since she would be in Sydney and he in Scotland, he had felt safe in giving that promise.

'Is it true that you were born on Flodday?' asked Donald.

'It is.'

'You don't look like a Flodday man.'

'What does a Flodday man look like?'

That stumped them. Like men everywhere, Flodday men were various.

'You know what I mean,' said Donald.

'I was born here in Kildonan. In Shore Street, in a house called Cruachan, where the roses always smelled of seaweed.'

So his mother had complained.

'It's still called that,' said Dugald. 'The McFarquars live there now.'

'So I've been told.'

'For somebody that's seen a lot of the world,' said Donald, 'you must find Flodday gey dull.'

'I find it beautiful. Beauty is never dull.'

'You can say that again,' said Torry, uneasily ogling the barmaid.

'Is that a good painting?' asked Donald, pointing to one on the wall above them. 'It's the bridge at Clachaig. Anybody could recognise it. So it must be good, mustn't it? Though I wouldn't give fifty quid for it.'

Beside the bridge was a wee white house, a few spindly trees, and some foxgloves, all daintily done. Angus had met the artist, a stout mannish lady of about 60, with short white hair.

'It's a pretty decoration,' he said, charitably.

'If you painted that bridge, it wouldn't look like it, would it?'

'You touch on matters profounder than you know.'

'We saw two of your pictures in the exhibition last summer.'

He had been asked and as a neighbourly gesture had agreed. It had been a mistake.

'One was called Sea Cliffs,' said Donald, 'but nobody thought it looked anything like sea cliffs.'

He paused then in his art criticism to join his friends in gazing at the barmaid's bottom, well displayed as she bent over a table to wipe off beer rings. Their lust was still subdued.

'I was good at drawing at school,' said Donald. 'I won a prize. When I drew something I tried to make it look like it.'

'So do I.'

'You must have funny eyesight.'

'If you painted a bridge,' said Dugald, 'it would be your idea of a bridge. Is that it?'

'It might also be my way of remembering my mother.'

They scowled, in sympathy.

'She's dead, isn't she?' muttered Dugald.

'Yes, she's dead, and buried in Kilnaughton graveyard.'

'My granny says she remembers your mother,' said Dugald. 'She was very cheery, she says.'

'So she was.'

Seeing that there was no one at the bar, Angus excused himself and went over to have his glass replenished.

'I didn't get your name,' he said.

'You didn't ask. It's Janet.'

'Janet what?'

'Janet Maxwell. Mrs. At present separated from Mr Douglas Maxwell.'

'Oh. My name's Angus McAllister.'

'I knew another Angus McAllister once. He was a wee fat man who kept a grocer's shop in Portree.'

Was this another demonstration of her second sight, maliciously intended? Had she divined that his name bothered him, by not having the ring of immortality?

'I'm told it's a fine big house you have at Ardnave?'

'It's a fair size.'

'I live here in the hotel. It's my cousin David's, or rather his wife's. You should see the room they've put me in. It's no bigger than a brush cupboard. It's far too stuffy. I can only sleep in a cool atmosphere.'

He could well believe it. She was as much a creature of the cold north as Fidelia was of the hot south.

'How would you like a lodger?'

He smiled, not taking her seriously.

'I'll be waiting outside the hotel tomorrow at eleven.'

More customers came in then and thronged the bar. He took his drink back to his seat.

Donald was wearing Angus's hat. He took it off.

'The barmaid, do you fancy her?' asked Torry.

'Better not,' said Dugald.

The three of them grinned.

Donald explained the joke. 'She's the kind would bite off your cock like the woman in the Bible.'

Angus could not recall any such woman, but perhaps they were right: Janet's place was not in Celtic mythology but the Old Testament, along with Lot's daughters, Delilah, Jael, Jezebel, and the apocryphal cock-biter.

2

Outside the bar the proprietor, David McNaught, Janet's cousin, a shy bald thin young man with a soft sure-as-death voice, waylaid Angus. He wore his usual uniform of black trousers, white shirt, and tartan bowtie.

'Could I have a word with you, Mr McAllister?' he whispered.

'Why not?' Angus supposed that he was going to be invited to display some of his paintings on the hotel walls.

'In my office, if you don't mind. It's rather confidential.'

'As you please.' As Angus followed him, he considered what prices he would demand. At least £200 a picture. But he had no intention of exposing his work to the insults of oafs like Donald and his pals.

On the desk in the small office was a stuffed penguin: all it needed to be a miniature of its owner was a tartan bowtie. Through the window was a view of the harbour. Live gulls could be heard screaming.

'Please sit down, Mr McAllister,' said McNaught. 'I'll not keep you long. I noticed you talking at some length to our new barmaid.'

'Barmaids are often loquacious.'

'She's my cousin.'

'Yes, she said so.'

'I don't know if you noticed or not, but I'm sorry to say she's on the verge of a nervous breakdown.'

It would explain the nonsense about second sight, and also the instinctive distrust of Donald and his pals.

'She's been enquiring about you, Mr McAllister.'

'So I gathered. I can't think why. We've never met before.'

'Well, you are quite a celebrity here.'

'Because of my painting?' That was sarcasm.

'Yes, of course, but there's the way you dress and then your house, with its strange contents. I'm afraid my daughters have been telling Janet about you. Jean's eight and Agnes is ten.'

Little ruffians sometimes cat-called him from around corners.

McNaught never smiled. Sometimes he came near it, as now. 'It isn't every house in Flodday that has a dragon painted on the ceiling, nor a life-sized Buddha in the living-room.'

'Please come to the point, Mr McNaught.'

'Janet, you see, has run away from her husband.'

'She said she was separated. When did it happen?'

'Just a week ago. Did she tell you why?'

'No, and I didn't ask.'

McNaught sighed again. 'I'm afraid it's rather a sordid story. I would like to ask your help, Mr McAllister.'

'How can I help? I don't know her husband, and I scarcely know her.'

'To cut a long story short, she came home unexpectedly from a holiday with her parents in Skye and found Douglas and a woman friend practising putting on the sitting-room carpet.'

'Quite a harmless if childish activity, surely?'

'They had no clothes on.'

'Not even gloves on their left hands?'

McNaught did not smile at what was quite a witty remark. 'I'm afraid Janet jumped to conclusions. She picked up one of the putters and hit him with it.'

Angus kept his face straight. 'On what tender spot?'

'She didn't say. It must have been painful for he lost his temper and struck her. He's a very strong man, a golfer and a karate expert. He could have broken her neck.'

14

She could have bitten off his cock. Angus still managed to look solemn.

McNaught then dropped his voice so low it was as if the penguin was speaking. 'Janet's not an ordinary kind of person. She has second sight.'

'So she said. I didn't believe her.'

'It's true. It's been in her family for generations. She had an aunt who was famous for it. People came from all over Skye to consult her. She went mad. We don't want that to happen to Janet. Do you believe in magic, Mr McAllister?'

Angus did. As a painter trying to portray and interpret the beauty of the earth and to convey the mysteries of the human soul, he had to believe in magic. But not in Janet's superstitious nonsense.

'Even as a child she was always imagining things. Her parents were very relieved when she married Douglas. He's a level-headed intelligent man.'

'Did you say he was a golfer?'

'A very good one, I understand. He wins cups.'

'In which case I am not so sure about his intelligence.'

'Douglas keeps his feet firmly on the ground.'

'Golfers must, I should say.'

'He's an engineer. Very practical. He once told me that he could spend a night alone in a graveyard without losing a minute's sleep.'

'I should think self-respecting ghosts would keep well away from a golfer. You mean, he's a clod, without imagination?'

McNaught winced, but nodded. 'Janet has a foolish notion that things will never be right between her and Douglas until he is made to realise there are more important things than golf or his new Rover.'

'Not so foolish, surely. Most wives would agree with her.'

'But most wives would not think that the way to bring that

about is for her to – well, misbehave (my word, not hers) with some stranger.'

'An eye for an eye, a tooth for a tooth, an adultery for an adultery. Sound Wee Free doctrine. I doubt though if it would make cloddish Douglas behave himself in future. He would be more likely to strike her again, harder this time.'

'She says she knows he will become more humble and more – mystical was the word she used.'

'Mystical?'

'It's a word she's fond of. I'm not quite sure what she means by it. She thinks that you, Mr McAllister, can help her cast the spell. Her words, not mine.'

'Me?' That was a squeal of indignation but there was amusement in it too.

'You see, you lived so long among black heathens and you have idols in your house.'

'I'm afraid, Mr McNaught, your cousin's not right in the head.'

'You wouldn't then, as an honourable man, take advantage of her?'

Angus rose. 'Wouldn't it be a case of her taking advantage of me? Good evening, Mr McNaught.'

As he made his way to his car, parked near the harbour, Angus consulted another soothsayer, a large gull watching him from the top of a mast, with mysterious yellow eyes. What painter, he asked it, would welcome the intrusion into his haven of a woman who claimed to have second sight, who believed in magic, who had run away from her husband, a quick-tempered karate expert, and who on the one hand was on the look-out for a sexual partner whose magic would match her own, and on the other hand was a suspected cock-biter? The gull stretched out its neck and opened its beak in a prolonged squawk. Wasn't he in need of company and inspiration? Didn't the woman in question meet his standards of beauty? Might not an affair with her galvanise him into producing powerful and enigmatic masterpieces? If that happened, no price would be too high to pay, not even a broken neck or bitten–off cock.

3

On Sunday morning Angus found himself driving slowly towards Kildonan, enjoying the splendid seascapes and identifying the many seabirds. He thought he saw a stormy petrel, a rare visitor. There was a place where on Sundays he liked to stop and listen to the church bells across the sea-loch. He could make out the white cottage where he had been born, so close to the shore that in winter the waves swamped the garden. Thus his mother had complained that her roses always smelled of seaweed, but she had laughed when saying it. In all his memories of her she was smiling, laughing, or singing. When he had sat by her death-bed she had smiled at him. That had been 33 years ago and he still missed her. He remembered too his father's grief. His father had died in Glasgow while Angus was abroad. Angus had flown home too late to see him alive but in time to have him buried in Kilnaughton graveyard beside his wife. There was room in the grave for Angus himself one day.

Amidst all the pleasant reassuring noises around him he heard his mother's cheerful voice: 'Dinna be sich a feartie, Angus.' But she had been encouraging him to wear a kilt in public, not to go and fetch a married woman who had run away from her husband. If he had heeded his mother's ghost, which was present in every sparkle of sunshine, he would have turned the car and gone back to Ardnave.

In any case, Janet was probably safe in church, listening to Mr McPherson's hour-long sermon, on the theme no doubt of the righteousness of retribution.

The Free Kirk minister had once called at Ardnave. He, who worshipped bloody-minded Jehovah, had been offended by the presence of Buddha, who had preached the sanctity of life. Angus had offered him a dram of Flodday Mist, the island's most famous malt and, to his surprise, it had been accepted. When Angus had gone out of the living-room for a minute or two he had come back to find the old minister looking through an illustrated book on the erotic sculptures of Hindu temples. He had been tempted to ask him if he would like to take it home for further study, but he had thought that Mrs McPherson, a dumpy little woman with a sour face, might see it and be outraged.

The loch was full of sunny spangles, but if a man ventured too far out he could drown. It should have been a warning.

Whistling, to propitiate, not defy, all the voices of nature urging him to go home, he started up the car and drove round the bay towards Kildonan.

Both kirks being in session, the streets were empty, stricken by a plague of piety. Shops were shut: they would be shut all day; a starving man would not be sold a loaf. Dogs and cats were imprisoned at home, lest their barking and miaowing should disturb the holy quiet. Even the gulls seemed to scream and squawk with less than week-day irreverence. At the pier no boys played with the boats tied up, and no fishermen mended ropes or nets. They were all in church, listening either to the Church of Scotland minister's parsimonious 20-minute sermon or in the Free Kirk, not a Bible's throw from Flodday Distillery, to Mr McPherson's harangue of an hour or longer.

As he rounded the corner before the hotel, Angus had still not decided what he would do if Janet was waiting for him, and there she was, seated on her suitcase on the hotel steps. Surprising himself, he felt compassion. If she really was in danger of mental collapse, where better to recover than at Ardnave, with its lambs and larks? He had not in his lifetime done so many deeds of kindness that he could afford to let this one pass. His motive would be misunderstood and maligned, but if his heart was pure, in this respect at least, he need feel no guilt.

He stopped beside her. She was wearing a red dress and white cardigan. Her hair was tied up with a red ribbon. Her legs were bare. She had on red sandals.

He had been visualising her as downcast but, on the contrary, she could not have been brisker and more self-confident. He had heard that people with mental troubles were either on a high or on a low, that was to say, either extravagantly cheerful or gloomily depressed. Janet, it seemed, was on a high.

He had not realised how beautiful she was. It was a beauty intense yet delicate, such as he had seen in paintings of medieval martyrs. If, like her aunt, she was to lose her sanity, a melancholy would be added. He must do his best to prevent that.

'Good morning,' he said, out of the window. 'I thought you would be in church.'

She rose. 'I was. But I slipped out. I had my case ready packed. I knew you would come.'

'Were you noticed slipping out?'

'Every head turned. Is your boot locked?'

He got out and helped her put the suitcase in the boot.

'Thanks,' she said, and was in the car before him. 'Let's go.'

'Right.' He would stop somewhere and have a serious talk with her.

As they passed Cruachan Cottage, he saw roses in the back garden. His compassion for his companion returned. For all her boldness she looked vulnerable.

'It's not true, is it,' she asked, 'that you don't like women?'

He felt cross. Was this how his kindness was to be rewarded?

'Is that what they have been telling you?'

'It seems the general opinion.'

About to reject scornfully that ridiculous slander, he fell into a deeper level of truth, perhaps because he had been thinking of his mother.

What really was his attitude to women? He did not mind their pettiness, their unpredictableness, or their unreasonableness. Such qualities, if not extreme, made for exhilarating intercourse. He had always played fair with them, making it clear from the outset that the relationship could not be permanent. Not even Fidelia had been excepted. In her case it had not been necessary. She was already married and, as a devout Catholic, ahborred divorce.

Why did he object to marriage? One simple reason was that he preferred sleeping alone. Even Fidelia's ample loving flesh, after an hour or so, had become oppressive. But then that had been in the tropics where even at midnight it was hot and sweaty. Still, many successfully married couples used separate beds, not to say separate rooms. Being an artist, he cherished his independence more than most men. He had painted the ceilings and walls of his house to please himself. No wife would have permitted those glorious excesses. Also, if he was doomed to failure as a painter he would be better able to endure it without wifely commiserations, whether sincere or not.

Those were the accessible reasons. There were others far below the surface. Was one of them his memory of his mother dying and his father weeping?

'Does it need all that thought?' asked Janet.

She had a way of staring. Was it her idea of coquetry, or did she think that was how a seer should look, or did she just need spectacles?

He stopped the car on a grassy bank close to the sea. Oyster-catchers pecked in the sand with their long red bills.

'We'd better talk about this,' he said.

'About what?'

'About your going to Ardnave. I'm not sure it's such a good idea.'

'I thought it was settled.'

'I never said I agreed. In fact I more or less promised your

22

cousin Mr McNaught to have nothing to do with you. What if your husband descended upon us?'

'He won't. He's in the wrong, so he won't.'

In Angus's experience people in the wrong were the worst troublemakers.

'Besides, he doesn't know where I am.'

'Won't your cousin tell him?'

'Not till Friday. That's our agreement. Anyway, he's often away from home on business. You needn't worry about Douglas. When he comes he'll be very humble.'

But not mystical, thought Angus.

'I'm a good cook. I'm sure after you've been painting for hours you'd like to find a nice meal waiting for you.'

Yes, but not with her bossing him about. He liked to relax after work, eating at leisure, with a bottle of wine, and listening to music.

'I'll pose for you. David was telling me you can't get models.'

'What about your job at the hotel?' said Angus, feebly.

'Oh that! I just did that for a laugh. Look here, I'm not proposing to stay with you for good. I wouldn't want that any more than you would. Just for a few days, that's all. I don't want to sleep with you either, if that's what's bothering you. I might ask you to make love to me, but it would be only once, and it would be for a particular purpose. If the conditions aren't right it won't happen. To tell you the truth, I'd be mortified if I was made pregnant by you, though we might have to take that chance. I want Douglas to be the father of my children. I love my husband but he's got to be made to understand that I'm not just a bit of elegant engineering. He'd much rather look at the Forth Road Bridge than the Mona Lisa. Because I've got second sight I sometimes see people who aren't really there. It may be they've been dead a long time, or it may be they've still to come, but I do see them. I can describe them and the clothes they're wearing. I've proved it to him but he refuses to believe. He says it's just hallucinations. He says what about all the times I've been wrong. Well, maybe I am wrong sometimes, but not often and there's always a reason. I shouldn't be telling you this, but he handles his new Rover with more care than he does me. I've told him he makes love like a crocodile. I cast up that he took more time in lining up a putt. Do you know what he said? He said a missed putt could lose him a championship. He wasn't joking either, not altogether. Now do you see why I've got to do something about him?'

It seemed to Angus nothing could be done about a golfing boor like Douglas, except perhaps fling his clubs into the sea, like so many Excaliburs.

It was Angus's turn to be psychic. He heard a faraway voice: Nell Ballantyne's. 'Jesus, Angus, here's a lady who'll give you a lot more trouble than ever I did. Before she's finished with you you'll be so mesmerised you'll not be able to paint worth a shit.'

That had long been a dread of Angus's, that one day when he picked up his brush his hand would have lost not only its cunning but also its power: however much he strove he would not be able to put the brush to canvas. It had already happened two or three times, but only momentarily. Nell, with her coarseness, had brought it about; and Fidelia more so, with her fits of remorse.

'Do you mind if I drive?' Janet was asking.

He should have said, 'Sorry,' and driven her back to the hotel, but he was already mesmerised.

'I like driving. I've got a red Mini at home. I've driven on Flodday before.'

They changed places and she set off, with what she would have called dash and skill, but what struck him as luck and recklessness. There was a drain to be cautiously avoided. She rushed over it with a bump, just missing a boulder that would have shattered the radiator. Back on the road, going much too fast in Angus's opinion, she met another car at a bend and shot

24

past it without braking, her off-wheels an inch or so from a deep ditch. The driver of the other car honked in shocked reproof. She retorted with several mocking toots.

If Angus had been, say, a schoolteacher or clerk, he would have begged her to take it easy. Being a painter eager to dispel timidity from his canvases, he just turned white and hastily fastened his seat belt.

If, he thought, the thousand million to one chance proved to be right and there *was* an after-life, would it not be galling if they crashed into a stone dyke or telegraph pole, and he, blameless more or less, went straight to the fires of hell, while she, culpably reckless, went to the flowers of heaven? But then he had always thought of hell as a place where good men nursed grievances, and of heaven as a place where villains couldn't believe their luck.

As they hurtled past the ruins of the ancient priory she remarked, as if talking about the weather, that on a previous visit to Flodday she and Douglas had made love there. She had hoped so hallowed and magical a place would have had an effect on him, but no, he had grumbled about the flies and midges and nettles. He had been wearing a kilt at the time.

Angus had never thought that he could ever feel sympathy for a golfer. Now he did feel a twinge for Douglas.

It was a relief when they left the public road with its stone walls and ditches and took to the sandy track that crossed the promontory. The worst she could do here was get cow dung on the tyres. On either side was machair, lush green grass and innumerable wild flowers. Charlie, the white Charolais bull, and his harem of Friesian cows were not in sight. Sheep were, though, with their lambs now as big as themselves, and rabbits, and little blue butterflies, and bees, and iridescent flies, and larks. On a warm sunny morning like this, Ardnave was Elysium.

'What a marvellous place!' cried Janet, as she got out of the car. 'Miracles could happen here.'

How could he contradict her? Was he not himself waiting for one, the turning of a competent, worthy, striving painter, whose kind were many, into a Master?

4

According to archaeologists, the site of Angus's house was where the living quarters of the priory monks had been. Their huts, made of wood, had long since crumbled into dust; but possessions of theirs had been dug up, nothing of gold or silver, for they had been poor from choice, but once, a small iron crucifix; this, with the rust of hundreds of years cleaned off, was now in the small museum in Kildonan, along with pieces of crockery. It had been established where their privy had been, a hollow in the bank near the sea. Today sea-flowers like thrift and campion and flag grew there in profusion. Angus had often imagined those peaceful men in their long brown inconvenient robes squatting there, reciting some appropriate prayer. He was sure they had not been without humour. In the gales and downpours of winter, much fortitude must have been needed. In spite of his civilised amenities, like septic tank and comfortable lavatory, he never felt any superiority over those humble, obscure predecessors of long ago. On the contrary he often felt consoled by them. He did not believe in God, and so all those hardships and prayers, in the service of God, had been in his view inevitably unavailing, but he could never think of them as wasting their time. Just as once, in the ruins at Angkor Wat in Cambodia, in a small chamber near the top, he had come upon two Buddhist monks in their saffron robes enjoying fly puffs at the one cigarette, with joss-sticks burning nearby in an Andrew's Liver Salts tin, and he had felt that, if there really was a God, they would have been nearer to Him than the gorgeously robed bishop he had seen conducting a service with pomp in a crowded church in Manila.

Sometimes, when faced with some moral problem, he would wonder what the monks would have advised. In one respect, however, they could be of no help: where women were concerned. They moved away whenever he was remembering his treatment of Fidelia. He had made use of her and then, when it suited him, he had let her down. He did not even know if he had loved her. He was not sure what love was. Nell too he had made use of, but then she had made use of him, so they had been quits. But Fidelia had given herself to him, though it had been for her a sin that, she knew, would send her to hell. God help him – if an agnostic could use that expression – he had looked upon her agonies of conscience not so much with a lover's sympathy as with an artist's curiosity. Only if he produced masterpieces could such colossal callousness be justified. He had produced one, her portrait. Justification, though, was still far from being achieved.

With these thoughts in his mind he watched Janet walking about, with gestures and cries of joy. She was taking possession of mysteries that were his, or was pretending to. In spite of her absurd claims to have psychic powers, she was really a disgruntled suburban Glasgow housewife whose husband was a dull fellow who played too much golf.

She lost no time in demonstrating how she intended to steal from him the magic of Ardnave. Looking down on to the little bay below the house she suddenly pointed and cried, 'Who are they?'

Dourly he went over and looked down. He saw only shells, three gulls, and some strands of seaweed on the pink sands, and at the far end two rocks covered with seaweed. 'I don't see anyone.'

'Two men. Old, I think. Wearing brown robes, kilted up. They're walking in the water. They're carrying their sandals. The tops of their heads are shining.'

'There's nobody there,' he said, crossly. 'Just rocks covered with seaweed.

'Rocks don't walk, do they?'

They did, if looked at through defective eyes or a self-deceiving mind.

He had often felt the presence of the monks, but never would again if this woman's childish nonsense drove them away.

He went closer to her and saw that she was trembling. She was paler than usual. She looked frightened. Her eyes, bluer than the sea-loch, had gone strange. He remembered her mad aunt. He thought of Douglas, again with sympathy. He touched her hand: it was icy cold. However spurious the apparitions, she certainly believed in them herself.

He noticed another odd thing. Flies did not seem to pester her as they did him. They buzzed about his eyes and ears but left her alone. It could be that she had washed her hair with some shampoo that luckily repelled them. That was a more rational explanation than that they were her familiars and she had some witch-like power over them.

She came out of her trance as quickly as she had gone into it. Once again a suburban housewife, interested in houses like all suburban housewives, she inspected his.

With its steep roof of blue slates and its solid doors painted dark blue, it was sometimes mistaken for a church. Indeed many of the whin stones used in its construction had been pilfered from the priory ruins. There was no man-made garden, but Angus regarded the whole machair, all the way to the precipitous cliffs overlooking the Atlantic where puffins nested, as his garden. No other house was in sight. His nearest neighbour, Mr McCandlish of Ardnave Farm, lived half a mile away, behind a green hill.

'You've got it in very good order,' said Janet. 'Did you have a lot to do to it?'

'Quite a lot. The roof had to be renewed.'

'Would it be too rude to ask how much you paid for it?'

He was not surprised by her mercenariness. Her Free Kirk upbringing explained that. But where had she got her notion that

29

lovers should be mystical? Douglas, with his crocodile single-mindedness, was more in keeping with the grim theology of Mr McPherson and his brethren.

'I paid fifteen thousand pounds for house and school. Repairs cost me another eight thousand.'

'Twenty-three thousand. It's worth double that now. Of course, it's not everybody would want to buy a place so isolated.'

'It wasn't always so isolated. There used to be a dozen crofts on the promontory. All derelict now. They must have had a hard time. Once thirty children attended the school. Just before it closed there were only two. I found the logbook in a cupboard.'

'Are you going to live here all your life?'

'Yes.' Even if the miracle did not happen, and, with age, he became a worse and not a better painter.

'It's all right now, when you're comparatively young; but when you're old it could be difficult living out here.'

'I have my protections.'

She then came upon one of them. 'What's this?' she asked.

It was his shrine. He had built it out of many-coloured many-shaped pebbles, with at the top an inverted scallop shell making a bowl in which every night he placed fragments of food, like the people of Bali, to propitiate demons that might otherwise bring harm to the house. Here, as there, birds or mice ate the grains of rice or crumbs of bread, but who was to say that feeding those innocent creatures was not pleasing to the demons?

Janet listened raptly. 'I hope you never forget to put out the food. What do you think would happen if you did?'

Nothing, he supposed. Yet . . .

'Is this another of your protections?' She meant the sheep's skull.

'Yes, though I didn't put it there. Some local youths did, for a joke.'

She laid her finger on the skull. It was her way of conciliating whatever magical forces were in it.

He opened the door. 'Here's another,' he said.

'You're well protected.'

The small vestibule was painted black, giving prominence to the large Balinese mask representing a demon's head, red, gold, and white, with big black bulging eyes, teeth like tusks, a lolling tongue of red cloth decorated with gold rosettes, and nostrils as wide as Charlie the bull's when he was pawing the ground.

'Rather a jolly demon, don't you think?' said Angus.

'It makes a good watchdog,' she said, and patted its head.

In the living-room was a smell of incense. Angus liked burning joss-sticks. Was it still another way of warding off evil?

Did he really believe that malevolent spirits existed?

Struck by the representations of demons to be found all over Bali, he had asked a professor at Denpasar University why spirits were always thought of as malevolent. The old man had replied that in his lifetime there had been earthquakes, floods, fires, epidemics, crop failures, and many deaths. Only when the spirits relented had there been rejoicing.

It had not occurred to Angus before that he had surrounded himself with so many protections. Even the yellow fire-spitting dragon he had painted on the ceiling could be seen as one, and the various small idols represented guardian deities. Chief of them all was the almost life-sized upright Buddha, in front of which Janet was now standing, frowning anxiously.

'I was told it was a thousand years old,' said Angus. 'To tell the truth, I suspect it was stolen from a museum.'

She was shuddering. 'I'm sorry, but there's something about this room I don't like.'

'Mr McPherson didn't like it either. Too many heathen idols.' he said.

'It's not that. It's something they can't stop.'

'He didn't like my divans either. He said he liked a chair to have a back and not be so near the floor. I told him you were supposed to sit on them lotus-fashion, with your legs crossed. He declined to try it.'

31

The three divans were red, yellow, and green, respectively.

'It's not your divans. I have a feeling that something terrible's going to happen here.' She pressed her hands against her head. 'I can't see what it is.'

She caught sight of his next most prized possession, after the Buddha: an authentic headhunter's blowpipe. It hung on the wall, with a bamboo quiver containing darts on one side and a vessel of bone 'for holding poison' on the other.

'The victim often never saw who had killed him. One puff and that was it. The poison on the dart paralysed him. Then he was stabbed to death by the spear-head at the end of the blowpipe. When it came to cutting off the head it was done with great reverence. It was a religious act, you see. The head was an offering to the gods.'

'Is it a real one? Has it ever killed anyone? I mean, it's not a fake made for tourists?'

'Look at it. It's at least a hundred years old. I bought it from an old chief. It was his father's. He had hundreds of heads hanging in his house.'

'It could still kill.'

'As a spear, I suppose it could. But the poison's all dried up.'

'I think you should take it down and hide it somewhere. Or burn it. Or throw it into the sea.'

'It's harmless now. The people it killed are all safely dead, thousands of miles away.'

'Nobody's safely dead,' she murmured.

He could have retorted, 'Not with you about.'

She picked up the book with the illustrations of erotic sculptures that Mr McPherson had found interesting. She opened it at random. There, looked in stony copulation, were the prince and his apsaras: on both their faces smiles of Nirvanic bliss.

'Do you know what Douglas would say? He would say if she's not careful she'll break her back.'

Well, considering he had the imagination of a crocodile.

She noticed writing in ink on the frontispiece: To Angus, with love, Fidelia.

'Who was Fidelia?'

'A colleague.'

'At the College?'

'Yes. She taught English.'

'But she wasn't British, with a name like that.'

'She was from the Philippines. She spoke excellent English.'

'Fidelia what?'

'Gomez.' Should he have said Dias, her maiden name?

'Sounds Spanish. Was she black?'

'No, she wasn't. A beautiful brown.'

All the same, she had kept out of the sun for fear of getting darker.

'She must have been more than a colleague for her to give you a book like that. Were you lovers?'

'Ask her yourself. She's upstairs in my bedroom.'

She was startled. 'I thought you lived here alone.'

'In a painting.'

'Oh. I'd like to see it.'

'All right.'

The staircase was wooden, painted white. He had amused himself decorating it with birds and butterflies in brilliant colours.

'You must have been feeling lonely,' said Janet the seer, stepping on butterflies. 'Which is your bedroom?'

He indicated it.

She opened the door and at once drew back, with a gasp. She was staring at Fidelia. 'My goodness!' she said, sounding like the suburban Glasgow housewife.

He still found it hard to believe that he had ever been able to find the boldness and panache to express in paint that vibrant sexuality. After all, he was at heart a puritan. Who born on

Flodday could avoid it? How had he managed to hit upon the right shade of brown, rich and glowing, like a polished chestnut! All the colours were vivid. The breasts large, round, and firm, as they had been; the belly round; the thighs plump; the waist too slender for the rest of the body, but that was how it had been; and the legs long and shapely. Among the sparse black pubic hairs a vertical red slash: a masterstroke. A hundred times, quailing, he had wanted to paint it out. The lips, full not thick, were the same eye-catching red. The hair long and jet-black. The eyes brown, honest, and sad. Where had he found the sensitiveness, let alone the skill, to paint those eyes?

It all amounted to a miraculous likeness.

'If it was in an art gallery with fifty other pictures everybody would look at it first,' said Janet. 'I don't know if that's a compliment or not.'

She went a little nearer. 'I feel I know her already.'

Outside a flock of oystercatchers flew past with shrill cries.

He could easily imagine Fidelia's soft worried voice, but could not think what she would have to say to him.

'Why have you made her so sad?'

'It was her nature.'

It was true that she had been prone to melancholy: a consequence, some said, of her headhunting ancestry. True enough, those wrinkled little black men, drunk with *tapai*, in their jungle huts adorned with many heads, could not have been very jolly.

'It would do Douglas good to see that picture,' said Janet. 'The women he has affairs with are all boring golfers with muscles. They talk golf all the time, and I mean *all* the time. Isn't making love supposed to be more spiritual than physical? Isn't it that which makes us superior to animals?'

She was being unfair to animals, thought Angus, or at any rate to Charlie the bull. *He* might lack spirituality but was always affectionate and attentive to his sweetheart of the moment, and never attempted her without making sure she was ready and willing. If he misjudged and was walked away from making him look foolish, he took it philosophically, apologised in his own way, and began all over again, with exemplary patience.

As for Douglas, what did Janet expect him to talk about to show that he was being spiritual? The works of St Thomas Aquinas?

In that activity silence was always safest. It was often just as well that the one participator did not know what the other was thinking.

Janet had picked up the photograph by his bed, of his parents and himself when he was about nine.

'That's you, isn't it? You were not sure of yourself even then.'

He let that pass. 'My mother was ill at the time.'

'Yes, she looks it.'

'She died not long afterwards. My father's dead too.'

'I can see he loved her very much.'

Yes, but there was no evidence of it in the photograph. His father was looking grim and anxious, not loving; but it was true, nothing was ever truer, he had loved her very much.

Angus had to keep tears out of his eyes.

Janet then went off on a tour of the other bedrooms. She chose one at the front with a view of the sea-loch. 'Would you bring up my suitcase, please? I'd like to change into jeans and walking shoes. They're more suitable if we're going to climb cliffs.'

He had said nothing about climbing cliffs.

5

When he was gone, puffing from the exertion of carrying her suitcase up the stairs, she opened it and took out the coloured photograph of Douglas. Where Angus's father looked anxious, as if afraid that his happiness was going to be taken away from him, Douglas looked self-assured to the point of cockiness, with nothing in the world, or out of it, threatening or daunting him. He scoffed when she told him what she had discovered with her second sight, that he was one of the lucky ones, favoured from birth; but it was true. He thought that his success, at golf and in his profession, was entirely owing to his own merits, but promotion had come to him more rapidly than to others equally hard-working and proficient, and he had beaten better golfers by what he himself called inspired play and his opponents a series of flukes.

It was a great disappointment to her that though an Elect he was utterly lacking in a sense of mystery. His golf clubs were his evidence that in inanimate things there was no magic: if a ball was well struck it travelled far and straight; if hooked or sliced it flew into the rough. And if people were sensible they would come to no harm: if they were foolish they deserved what they got.

He considered golf not only a game but a religion – did it not have a book of rules as thick as a Bible? – and if he put love-making on the same level of importance, what was she complaining about? The trouble was, she found it hard to explain what she wanted from him as a lover. When she had called him a crocodile, she had not been referring to his demands on her when she was not in the mood – though no doubt female crocodiles were crawled upon without being asked – nor to his grunts, nor the smell off his breath, whisky in his case usually, rotten meat perhaps, in the crocodile's, nor the abrupt endings just when she was arranging some romantic situation in her mind, nor his going to sleep immediately afterwards, with snores of contentment. What she had meant was his belief that a woman who enjoyed love-making, or even wanted to enjoy it, was immoral. He had claimed to have read that in the Bible somewhere.

A crocodile, whatever its attitude to its offspring, made no attempt to prevent their conception. Douglas did not want children until he was 30. What could be more disenchanting than the furtive slipping on of a contraceptive?

If he had been an ordinary man, like his fellow golfers, she would have borne her disappointment, as golfers' wives had to bear theirs. She had not expected him to perform miracles or have a golden umbilicus or be extraordinary in any obvious way, but she had looked for some spiritual quality, and so far had looked in vain.

When she had surprised him and Cissie McDade in the sitting-room practising putting, with no clothes on, what had disgusted her most was how silly, cringing, and common he had looked, like any other man caught in the same circumstances.

If he had stood up boldly, like a Greek hero, his hand his fig leaf, and with his other hand pointed the putter at her like a magic wand such as Perseus might have possessed, she would not have gone down on her knees exactly, nor would she have forgiven him without his doing penance, but in her heart she would have admired and adored him. As it was he had let her grab the putter from him and hit him on the left shin with it. The blow he had struck her in retaliation had been that of a lamed golfer, not of a Chosen One roused to wrath.

38

Here he was, in the photograph, smiling at her brazenly, his brown hair expensively coiffured and his little moustache neatly trimmed. His blue blazer with the golf club crest on it in gold, and his tie to match, and his white shirt, were all the best money could buy. If his after-shave could have been smelled, it would have overcome the fragrance of incense now strong in the room. If his hands had been visible, his cufflinks would have been seen to be of gold, and his fingers expertly manicured. He patronised an establishment whose assistants were nubile young women in thin pink overalls.

She put the photograph on the dressing-table, and then began to rummage through the drawers. Douglas would have rebuked her. He was a staunch respecter of other people's property, in order that they would respect his. It was easy for him really, because he wasn't interested in other people or their property. Janet, on the contrary, even as a child, had been interested in other people's lives; indeed she had been accused of trying to run them.

In one of the drawers she came upon, wrapped in tissue paper, two feminine garments, one a sleeved blouse, the other a long skirt, both red with black designs. She had seen pictures in magazines of Eastern women wearing clothes like these. Was the skirt called a sarong? There was a perfume off them, musky but not unpleasant. She was sure they had belonged to Fidelia. She soon found that they could well have, so far as size was concerned, for, quickly stripping to bra and pants, she put them on, finding the blouse too wide across the bosom and the skirt too slack across the buttocks. In spite of their poor fit, the strange clothes made her feel strange. She was no longer Janet Maxwell, suburban housewife, who lived in a semi-detached villa called Blaven in Clarkston, did the washing on Monday, the hoovering on Tuesday, the supermarket shopping on Wednesday, other shopping on Thursday, was taken on Saturday evening to a golf-club function, and on Sunday went to church with her next-door neighbour Maggie Brown, whose husband also was a golfer. She was instead a hostess in a night-club in Manila, entertaining swarthy millionaires. Wailing music coming up from below and the smell of incense gave backing to her fantasy.

There she was, hardly herself, far away in imagination, when suddenly a fit of second sight came upon her: her scalp turned icy cold. Forced to the window, she looked out. On the grass in front of the house was a tall woman she recognised as Angus's Fidelia, though she was wearing European dress, a blue coat with a white skirt under it. There was someone with her, a small girl of about ten, whose face and legs looked all the darker because of her white coat and the white ribbon in her hair. Though they were visions they were as clear as the ewe that ran past, with its two lambs.

The woman was Fidelia, but who was the little girl? Was Angus reluctant to talk about his relationship with Fidelia because they had had a child? It would account for his evident feelings of shame – he must have deserted the child – and also for his providing himself with so many guardians. Several times Janet had been about to ask him what he was afraid of. Had she now found out?

She shut her eyes. When she opened them again, the apparitions had gone.

She had to sit down on the bed, so weak were her legs.

Should she tell Angus that Fidelia was coming, and bringing their daughter with her? He would not want to believe her but when they did come he would be prepared.

He was calling up that lunch was ready.

She changed into jeans and went down.

He had been busy. The table was set in the dining-room. There were plates of chopped melon, coconut, banana, pineapple, lettuce, and tomato. A bottle of white wine stood in a pewter bucket full of water.

'I hope you like curry,' he said. 'Malayan. Not as hot as Indian.'

40

'It smells very nice.'

'Would you like a sherry?'

'No thanks. I don't drink.'

She had to tell him. She had to pass on the message. That was why it had been given to her.

'Has Fidelia got a sister?'

'I'd rather not talk about her.'

'But I have to. I saw her, just five minutes ago, outside the house. She had a little girl with her.'

She read his face. He was annoyed with her for talking about Fidelia and he was trying to remember if he had told her about the little girl.

'They're coming here,' she said.

'Those two monks you said you saw, are they coming here too?'

'They're different. They're here all the time. Who is the little girl? Is she your daughter, yours and Fidelia's?'

'No, she isn't.'

'But she's Fidelia's. They looked like mother and daughter.'

'She's Fidelia's. Fidelia's married, or I should say has a husband. She hasn't seen him for years. He lives in Manila. He owns night-clubs and brothels. Letty's his daughter.'

She frowned, thinking he was making fun of her. 'You're joking aren't you, about him being the owner of brothels?'

'Vice is a lucrative trade in the Philippines. It is also respectable.'

'Have you ever met him?'

'No. Now shall we sit down and enjoy lunch?'

They sat down.

'If he's so nasty and she hasn't seen him for years, why doesn't she get a divorce?'

'She's a devout Catholic. She does not believe in divorce.'

'Is that why you left her behind?'

He did not answer.

41

'I'm sorry, Angus, but I had to tell you. They're coming here, very soon; perhaps today or tomorrow.'

'Let me say, you believe you saw them in some absurd vision, but there's no reason why *I* should believe you. Let's talk about something else. Douglas, if you like.'

6

During lunch Angus was huffy and depressed. Janet wondered if it was because of the news she had given him. Since she drank none of the wine, he drank it all. It had the effect of causing him to talk, not about Douglas, but about painting. She had not realised as she should have how important it was to him. He did not actually say it but it was implied in half-a-dozen things he said, that being married would cripple him as an artist, though it might benefit him as a man. She was not sure whether or not to sympathise with him.

'I've only seen one of your paintings,' she said. 'The one upstairs. I think it's very good, but I don't suppose I'm a good judge. Have you ever sold any?'

'In Basah I sold more than a hundred.'

'My goodness! What was the most you ever got for a painting?'

'Two hundred pounds.'

She was impressed. 'If you were to do three a week – and that wouldn't be so hard, would it? – you'd make more than Douglas.'

'More than diligence is required.' He spoke bitterly.

'What was it about, the painting you got two hundred pounds for?'

'Three Chinese whores, on the balcony of the bar where they worked.'

'Not a very nice subject. Who bought it?'

His bitterness increased. 'A man who did not like me. He was prepared to pay two hundred pounds to show his contempt for me. He and his golfing cronies used it as a dartboard.'

'Why did he throw away his money like that?'

'I was having an affair with his wife.'

'Well, what could you expect?'

'He was a notorious womaniser himself. He corrupted girls half his age.'

'Did he work at the College too?'

'He was in the timber business. Basah is covered with forests. An Australian. With typical beer-belly.'

'What was his wife like, that you had an affair with?'

'Would you like to see her?'

'Yes, I would. Did you paint all your lovers?'

'If the affair lasted long enough.'

'You're talking as if you had a lot. Would you believe it if I was to tell you that Douglas is the only man I've ever made love with?'

'Yes, Janet, I would believe it.' He grinned. 'Are you finished? Shall we go and look at Nell?'

He led the way to his studio, which had once been the schoolroom. There were paintings stacked all round the walls. On an easel was his work in progress.

Janet stared at it, dubiously. 'What's it supposed to be?'

'Mist on water.'

She frowned, as schoolmistresses had often done in that very room to wrong-headed pupils. 'Where's the one of your sweetheart Nell?'

He let the term pass. Sweetheart denoted some degree of docility. Nell had been the most rumbustious of lovers.

He knew where to find her portrait among all the other canvases. He looked at it quite often: not because he missed Nell so much but because it pleased him as a painting. He had taken risks in it. He thought they had come off, though others, including Nell herself, had not.

44

He put it up on the easel.

Admitting that she knew 'fuck-all' about art Nell had never taken any of his painting seriously. This portrait made her look, she had said, like a female orang-utan begging for a banana. This, he supposed, was because he had, deliberately, exaggerated the redness and abundance of her hair, on head and body; and also because he had tried to depict an elusive wistfulness which had not sat well on her damn-you-all features.

'Did she really have all that red hair?' asked Janet.

'Her hair was beautiful.'

'On her head maybe, but not there surely.'

Prudish bitch, he thought. But he smiled bravely. She was entitled to her opinion.

'Well, you would know, wouldn't you?' she said, being smutty this time. 'She looks vulgar. Was that just the way you painted her or was she really vulgar?'

'She was honest. Some people thought she expressed her opinions too frankly.' He had been one of them.

'I must say, Angus, she doesn't look your type.'

Many had said so. What had fat boozy foul-mouthed good-hearted Nell Ballantyne seen to admire and like in prim, selfish Angus McAllister? And, of course, vice versa.

Well, setting aside the malicious unfairness of those descriptions, what had been the attraction between them? He could speak only for himself. Himself unwilling or perhaps unable to give much of himself to anyone, he had been fascinated by Nell's openness and generosity. Also he had soon discovered that beneath her outward swagger there was a vulnerability that not many knew about: it had put her in his power. But, above all, he had got from her sex without responsibility, which every creative artist needed. Rather a finicky lover himself, he had found in her ample embrace all his Calvinistic reservations being swept away, so that he emerged exhausted as a man, but liberated as an artist.

45

If this inquisitive suburban housewife beside him was to ask which of the two, Nell or Fidelia, he had loved more, he would not have known what to say. In spite of the menace in the background of her brawny husband Bruce, he had found Nell's love-making more fruitful to him as an artist, which was really all that mattered. Fidelia had given herself body and soul; but that had been the trouble, he had not wanted her soul and its agonisings. He had loved her more deeply than he had Nell or any other woman, she was the only woman for whose sake he had shed tears, but he had known all the time, every minute of all the time, that one day he would be glad to leave her behind. Even if she had not been married or had been divorced, he would never have asked her to marry him. He could have overcome his instinctive prejudice against her colour and he could have accepted little Letty as his step-child, but there were other things, only vaguely understood, that had deterred him. Put simply, he had been too much of a coward to take Fidelia and Letty home with him.

Meanwhile Janet had been looking at more of his paintings. By this time she had seen enough.

'Well, shall we go and wash the dishes?' she said, in her role of suburban housewife, and then added, as the Old Testament doom-bringer, 'After that we'll go and climb the cliffs.'

7

For the walk across the promontory to the Atlantic cliffs, Angus
took a knapsack with sandwiches and a flaskful of whisky, just in
case. He also carried binoculars with which to study the seabirds,
which were multitudinous on the cliffs, and to keep an eye on
Charlie the bull. He needn't worry, Janet remarked, bulls
weren't dangerous if they were with cows.

Ardnave that afternoon was at its most magical. The immense
sea-meadow sloped up gently, so that walking on the springy turf
was easy and delightful. The air was warm but not enervating,
and it was fragrant with the scent of many thousands of little wild
flowers. Bees buzzed and small blue butterflies fluttered. In the
sky larks sang unceasingly, and from the beach curlews kept
calling. Sheep and lambs were everywhere, galloping out of the
way with sour bleats. Away in the distance Charlie and his harem
could be seen; an occasional lowing was heard.

Janet soon broke into a Gaelic song about a girl herding cattle.
Angus at first joined in but had to give up because of the flies.
They rose in hordes from cowpats and bumped against his lips;
one indeed got in his mouth and had to be spat out. As an artist
he was bound to admire the iridescence of some and the bright
blueness of others, but it did not quite compensate for the
irritation they caused, especially as his companion was again
immune. Only one or two went near her and were easily waved
away. At last he asked, with a forced jocularity, how was it that
they pestered him but not her. She replied that perhaps it had to
do with the kind of skin and blood she had. A red-haired fair-

skinned person like his friend Mrs Ballantyne, particularly if she had got fat, and she was the sort that would, would be driven mad by clegs and midges, so it was just as well that she wasn't coming here. Ah, he said, sarcastically, so there had been no prophetic vision relating to Nell? No, there hadn't been, not yet anyway.

Their way took them up and down across several natural amphitheaters, sheltered from the breeze and therefore very warm. The ground was one great mattress of sand, grass, feathers, tufts of wool, flowers, sheep's pellets, and cowpats. Here, mused Janet, would do very well for her purpose, which was to entice Angus into making love to her, not for her own sake or for his but for Douglas's.

If she was ever to shock Douglas out of his golfer's view of things, as good a way as any would be for her to be in a position to tell him that she had made love with another man. That other man would have to be someone unusual. A golfer would not do. Angus, being an artist, would do very well. Douglas had decided all artists were frauds, after a visit to an exhibition of Picasso's paintings. If she was to tell him that she had been unfaithful to him with an artist with a beard, his thoughts and emotions, all carefully in place, like his shirts and suits in his wardrobe at home, would be scattered like a flock of sheep disturbed by a dog. He would whimper that if it had been her intention to get her own back she ought to have borne in mind that, while a man's extra-marital adventures did his wife no harm, a woman's could leave her husband with a child that wasn't his. If that was unfair, don't blame him, blame biology. But when his bluster had died away, he would never be the same self-satisfied, cocksure, know-all young man again. He would have learned about mystery. She thereafter would love him all the more.

For his part, Angus was thinking, amidst his cloud of flies, that her ploy might be to have an affair with him. After all, he would be a big improvement on her golf-crazy bully of a husband. His objection to any affair was that it might not be so easily ended as in Basah. There, where contracts might or might not be renewed, everything from membership of the yacht club to possession of a mistress had been necessarily temporary. Even his love for Fidelia had been a commitment with a foreseeable end. Either he or she or perhaps both of them would have to leave one day and return to their respective native country. In the event it had been he. As far as he knew, she was still in Basah and they would never see each other again. But if he entered upon an affair with Janet, say, there would be no such inevitable limit imposed by circumstances. Beautiful though she was, he would one day grow tired of her, but when he suggested, in a civilised manner, that it was time for her to go, she might rudely refuse. Much safer to let her return unblemished to her Douglas.

In half an hour or so, their shoes yellow with pollen, they reached the 200-feet-high cliffs and gazed out at the blue Atlantic. Though he exulted like Xenophon, Angus did not venture too near the edge, for, besides having a poor head for heights, he trusted neither the turf undermined by puffins nor his companion's sanity. Crazy people, he reflected, threw themselves over; half-crazy ones pushed others over.

Like a madwoman indeed, Janet was screaming about cliffs in Skye twice as high as these. 'We used to climb them gathering gulls' eggs.'

'Liar,' he muttered, childish in return.

Far below was a small bay all the more alluring because inaccessible. Breakers as big as houses fell in leisurely order on white sand: the sound, a roar like cannon, came seconds later. Off-shore were rocks on which cormorants sat and from which spray rose shot with rainbow colours. It was the sort of secret place where a selkie, or seal woman, of Gaelic legend might come ashore. She would be safe there, for though there was a possible route of descent, which he had discovered on previous visits, only a madman would attempt it. Studying it through

49

binoculars, he had concluded, as he did now, that with un-remitting effort and care, and at the cost of a few bruises and cuts and many frights, that slope of scree at the top, those slabs of stone, green and slippery with slime, and that long fissure, could all be descended, for none was quite vertical and there were tufts of heather and thrift and knobs of rock to hold on to, and plenty of ledges to rest a foot on. Nevertheless a stumble or slip that on flat ground might cause a jarred ankle could mean here a precipitate downward plunge, with bones broken, blood spilled, and in all likelihood life extinguished.

'Give me the binoculars,' cried Janet. 'I think I see a way down.' She scanned the cliff. 'Yes, there is. Look.'

'I've already looked.'

'We could get down there, couldn't we? It's never as steep as it looks.'

'Famous last words.'

They had to shout because of the din made by the seabirds flying about in their thousands.

'Wouldn't it be marvellous to walk on those sands?' she cried.

'It's just as marvellous walking on sands that you don't have to risk your life to reach.' But he didn't really believe that.

'If Douglas was here he'd tackle it like a shot. He's afraid of nothing.'

Angus was reinforced in his wish never to meet the bump-tious, unimaginative Douglas.

'Are you coming?' she asked.

'I certainly am not.'

'Then I'll go alone.'

He felt sorrier for himself than for her. If she was killed he would be blamed. They would say that he had known her to be of unsound mind and yet he had brought her to this dangerous place.

She had already begun, sliding down the scree on her backside.

Judging from their concerted screams, the birds seemed to share Angus's opinion of her recklessness.

He did not want to watch but felt obliged to: if she met with disaster, at least he could share it to the extent that he saw it. Lying on his stomach, he looked through the binoculars.

Her light blue jeans and white blouse were already smeared with green slime. She was on her bottom a good part of the time but in steeper places she had to face the cliff, like a rock climber, and feel with her foot for a ledge. Two or three times she slipped and only stopped herself by grabbing at some vegetation. Once she let out a scream. Halfway down she rested a while, as if trying to decide whether to keep going or turn back. She kept going. It began to seem that if her luck held she would make it; but she had still to get back up, a harder and riskier task.

At long last, after 35 minutes, she was safely down. He envied her as she walked across the sand. The magic of the place was hers. Perhaps no other human being had walked there in the past one hundred years. It was more marvellous than walking on the moon. There the imagination would have been stifled by the nothingness, but down on those remote sands she was in the midst of many enchantments. The birds were now screaming congratulations. Angus himself murmured: 'Well done.'

She undressed, throwing her clothes about the sand. Then she raced into the sea, disappearing in a welter of bright water. Had the selkie gone back to her own kind? No, there she was again, glistening with wet.

He noticed what she did not seem to be aware of, that her clothes were in danger of being reached by one of the long tongues of the sea. Worse still, she herself could be cut off.

He shouted a warning but the birds' incessant screaming and the sea's roar drowned it.

If it had been Nell Ballantyne dancing about down there, even Nell as she had been eight years ago, she would have looked fat and clumsy by comparison. Fidelia, as graceful but less agile, would not have enticed his imagination so much. She would not have looked at home down there, beside that cold sea. She was a creature of the warm south. Flodday would never have suited her.

Aware now of the sea's approach, Janet was putting on her clothes. He shivered in sympathy for they must be soaked. He should be climbing down to meet her and give her help, for she would be stiff with cold and therefore more likely to fall. He stayed where he was, with the excuse that he would be more of a hindrance. Was it necessary for an artist to be courageous as a man? If it was, he might as well give up painting. But would Rembrandt, at the age of 43, have scaled that cliff?

It took her nearly an hour to reach the top. He half expected her to brush aside his hand held out but no, she took it, gratefully, and also his flask of whisky, though she said, with chittering teeth, that she detested whisky.

'Let's find a warm hollow,' she said, 'where I can take off my clothes.'

They did not have far to go to find a cosy hollow, like a nest, lined with feathers, wool, grass, and violets. Janet at once took off her clothes and wrung them out. She handed Angus her jeans to do. Then, with sheep's pellets sticking to her white bottom, she stood up and spread out her garments to dry.

'Have you got anything I could dry myself with?' she asked.

In his knapsack he had a woollen cap. He gave it to her.

She dried herself all over. 'I expect, as a painter, you'll have seen lots of women with their clothes off?'

He nodded.

'That's all right, then. I'm going to sunbathe for a while. I feel tired. You can go for a stroll if you like.'

'I think I'll take a rest too.'

'Do you still want me to model for you?'

'Yes.'

'Well, I'll do it if you'll do something for me in return.'

'What, for instance?'

'Make love to me.'

He had opened his eyes but now he shut them again. Never had he felt less lustful.

'What about Douglas?' he jeered.

'It would be for his sake that I would be doing it.'

Suddenly aware of another danger, he opened his eyes and looked up.

Glaring down, with a copper ring through his nose and a white cloud sitting on his head was Charlie the bull, swishing his tail, which could have been to swipe away flies, and pawing the ground, which could have been to stamp on ants, but both activities seemed more likely to indicate resentment at finding a favourite nook usurped. He did not roar but his grunts were just as intimidating. A black-and-white cow appeared at his side, licking his sharny rump.

'Look out!' cried Angus.

Janet opened her eyes. 'What's the matter?'

From where she lay she could not see Charlie's virile tuft but his ring and bloodshot eyes were enough. Showing no faith in her own dictum that a bull with a cow was not dangerous, she gathered up her clothing and fled.

Angus had previously been introduced as it were to Charlie by the farmer and had even patted the brute's massive head. 'A peaceable beast, Mr McAllister, so long as you leave his coos alane.' Mr McCandlish had chuckled; he put nothing past a man who had heathen statues in his house. 'It's all right, Charlie,' said Angus, in a soothing but shaky voice. Charlie glowered, snorted, and seemed minded to charge. Instead he turned away and began tearing up grass, not because he was enraged but because he had resumed grazing.

Picking up binoculars and knapsack, Angus made off after

Janet, but not in panic. Seldom had he felt more fearless. Metaphorically speaking, he could have climbed a cliff ten times as high or faced a hundred fierce bulls. He had had an inspiration for a painting.

8

From about 200 yards away Janet, clothed again, could see a car outside the house, parked beside Angus's. It was David's. He must have come to take her back. She hoped Mary wasn't with him, or Mr McPherson. Thanks to Charlie the bull she would be able to say with truth and therefore with conviction that she had not sinned with McAllister. She would also be able to say with equal truth that she had no intention of doing so. She still had faith in her theory of therapeutic shock in regard to Douglas but she would have to find some other way of administering it. Having McAllister make love to her, she now realised, would have given *her* a shock by no means therapeutic. She could, of course, pretend it had happened. Only Angus would be hurt by the lie, but only if he knew and she certainly wouldn't tell him. Douglas though, as a consequence of his shock, might go rushing out to Ardnave and give Angus a hammering. Well, perhaps Angus deserved one for the way he had treated Nell and Fidelia and other women too.

She waited till Angus made up on her, puffing and panting, but in a curious state of exaltation. His eyes glittered as if he had just gained something wonderful and not lost it. Though she had never made love to any man but Douglas, she had attracted many lecherous glances at golf-club dos and more than once had had her bottom squeezed. She might not be as sexy as Fidelia or as cuddlesome as Nell but she was not repulsive either. Angus therefore ought not to be looking so pleased. Could it be that he was looking forward to doing in his bed what he had just missed doing in the grassy hollow? No, *that* wasn't the kind of smile he had.

'David's come for me,' she said. 'Look, that's his car.'

He grabbed her arm but with no sexual intent. His mind was on something loftier.

'You mustn't go back,' he cried. 'You promised to pose for me. I've had an idea for painting. I need you for it.'

'Probably all Kildonan's talking about me.'

'What does that matter? It'll be the biggest and most ambitious painting I've ever done. I know I can bring it off. It's what I've been waiting for. Tell McNaught you can't go back. Not till Wednesday. Tell him you'll go back on Wednesday.'

Well, perhaps her staying in Angus's house for three nights unchaperoned would be enough to give Douglas his salutary shock. Besides, she would want to be at Ardnave when Fidelia and the little girl arrived.

'All right, I'll stay till Wednesday, at least. But let me speak to David.'

Approaching the house she skipped and danced in a way that she hoped David would associate with his daughters Jean and Agnes and therefore with carefree innocence. But the face with which he confronted her was gloomy as Jeremiah's.

Angus gave him a nod and then hurried into the house.

'What's the matter with him?' muttered David, suspiciously.

'I think he wants to start a painting. He's had an inspiration.'

'I just hope his inspiration had nothing to do with you.'

'I think it had to do with a bull called Charlie.'

'Why is your hair wet, and why are your jeans so dirty?'

'I was climbing a cliff. Don't worry, David, Mr McAllister and I have done nothing wrong.'

'Would you swear by Sgurr Alasdair?'

That was a secret oath of childhood: a guarantee of truth.

'I swear by Sgurr Alasdair.'

56

David's gloom hardly decreased. 'I believe you, but nobody else will. Douglas won't.'

'I don't want Douglas to believe me. I want him to think I've misbehaved with Angus. He's got to be given a jolt. He's got to be made understand that there are more important things than golf.'

'That's nonsense, Janet. He's more likely to assault McAllister.'

'Well, that would be all right. McAllister deserves it. Not because of anything he did to me, but because of what he did to other women. I suppose Mary's telephoned Douglas?'

'She tried but he wasn't at home.'

'He'd be out looking for comfort from one of his lady-friends.'

'She's going to try again this evening. I'm afraid she'll tell him about Mr McAllister. So he'll probably arrive on tomorrow's plane.'

'No, he won't. He won't believe her. He'll just laugh. What a joke, his Janet doing what he's often done himself. His Janet's not that kind of woman. She was too well brought up. Her parents have been members of the Free Kirk all their lives. That's what he'll tell himself. He'll not come tomorrow. He'll wait till Saturday and bring his golf clubs.'

'But there's no need for you to stay here till then. Mary said I'd to bring you back with me.'

'Mr McAllister's expecting guests. He wants me to help him receive them.'

'What guests? Do you know them?'

'People he knew in that place abroad: Basah. A woman and her daughter.'

'Isn't the woman's husband coming too?'

'No. Well, I think you should be getting back, David. Mary will be getting anxious. Give my regards to her and the girls.'

'All right, but I don't like it.' He went off to his car with a last sigh.

★　　★　　★

She went into the house and found Angus in his studio, hard at work. He hardly noticed her coming in or standing by his side. He seemed to be planning the picture. She made out the outlines of a bull and a woman. There were also cliffs, clouds, and birds, roughly sketched but recognisable.

'David's gone,' she said.

'Good.'

'I think I can stay till Saturday.'

'There's no need. I should be finished with you by Wednesday.'

She could have kicked him. 'All the same I'll stay till Saturday. I'd like to meet your visitors.'

He grunted.

'I expect Douglas will come on Saturday.'

Another grunt.

'Well, if I'm in the way I might as well go and make the tea.'

'Do that.'

'What's in the larder?'

'Look and see.'

She should have been annoyed with him and yet she wasn't. He was doing what he wanted to do more than anything else in the world. She envied him therefore but, what surprised her, she pitied him too.

She had to come three times and tell him tea was ready. He gobbled down his scrambled eggs and toast like a dog and grunted when she spoke to him. The moment he was finished he rushed back to his studio.

What if, she thought, after all this devotion, concentration, and rudeness, the picture produced was a failure? She herself wouldn't be able to tell, but he would. It must be dreadful to have to tell yourself that a painting which at the start you thought was going to be a work of genius was after all no better than dozens of others you had done.

About nine o'clock she looked in and asked if he had noticed the beautiful sunset. The loch was blood–red. She was going out to have a good look at it. Would he like to come?

He shook his head. Yet he wasn't working. Just thinking. She hadn't realised that a painter might have to think long and hard about a painting, like an author writing a book.

When she came in, driven from the glory in the sky by midges – her immunity seemed to have lapsed – Angus was in the living-room squatting on the red divan, silent and meditative, as if imitating Buddha, except that he was drinking Flodday Mist. She sat on the green divan, cross-legged, as if imitating him.

That meant, in the shadowy room, three Buddhas. The head of the one standing was touched with red from the dying sun: so was the blowpipe. She still had a feeling that something terrible was going to happen in this room, but it seemed so peaceful now and so well guarded that she thought her psychic powers must have deceived her. It would not be the first time.

'This picture,' she said, 'what's it going to be about?'

'You'll see when it's finished.'

'I'm not so sure about that. Douglas and I once went to an exhibition of Modern Art and we didn't understand a single one of the pictures.'

'No doubt. I'd like to start early tomorrow. The light's best then. Could you be ready at eight?'

'Ready for what?'

'To be my model.'

'Won't it be still chilly then?'

'You'll be fully clothed.'

'Oh.' She couldn't have said why but she felt disappointed.

He got to his feet, stiffly. 'If you don't mind, I'm going up to bed. You must be tired too.'

So she was, and her bruises were aching. 'I'd like to take a hot bath first.'

The water was heated by gas. It took nearly an hour to heat a bathful. Sometimes the water was the colour of peat.

59

She heard him going up the stairs.

'Did you remember to put out the food for the demons?' she called, half joking.

He stopped. 'Will you do it?'

'They don't know me.'

He came back down and went into the kitchen for some bread.

'I was joking,' she said. 'I would have done it.'

'No, it's my job.'

Douglas would have scoffed at them both, as superstitious idiots. She would have been cross with him for denying the magic, and yet she would have found his presence reassuring.

Perhaps Douglas was right. The time for magic was childhood and she was no longer a child. He himself boasted that he had stopped believing in Santa Claus when he was three.

9

Next morning Janet opened her eyes to find Angus staring not at her but at Douglas in the photograph. He was dressed for outdoors.

'Is that Douglas?' he asked.

'Yes. Why?' She was only half awake.

'I wondered what he looked like. I suppose he's big and strong.'

'He's six feet and twelve-and-a-half stone. What's this about? He hasn't come, has he?'

'No.'

'What time is it?'

'Seven o'clock. I'm going out to do some sketching. I won't be back for lunch. I'm taking sandwiches and a flask.'

'I thought you were going to paint me this morning.'

'Tomorrow will do, since you're going to be here till Saturday. It's a fine morning. I've got to take advantage of it. It could be raining tomorrow.'

'What are you going to sketch?'

'Cattle, mainly.'

'Would you like me to come with you?'

'No. You would be bored.'

'Won't it be dangerous on your own?' There were no trees on the machair to climb or hide behind. She almost said that he ought to be back by twelve to greet Fidelia and Letty. The plane landed on Flodday at eleven. The taxi bringing them to Ardnave would take little more than half an hour.

'I'll be back about three,' he said.

She heard him running down the stairs. All that urgency and dedication, she thought, to paint a picture that, to be truthful, not many people would think worth looking at. It seemed that not only great painters had to work very hard to produce their masterpieces, so had ordinary ones to produce their mediocrities. Douglas believed that with the invention of coloured photography painting had become unnecessary. When she had reminded him that some paintings fetched millions of pounds at auctions he had said yes, so they did, but as investments not as things of beauty.

Was Angus, user of women, timid, self-centred and self-satisfied, capable of creating a thing of beauty? She did not know enough about the great painters of the past to tell if they had all been brave, considerate, and gentlemanly, but she wouldn't be surprised to learn that they had not. So Angus had as good a chance as any to paint a great picture, provided he had the talent. But why had he been interested in Douglas's photograph? She wished him good luck and went to sleep again.

She got up shortly after nine and went downstairs to make herself breakfast. Passing Angus's room, she saw that the bed had been neatly made. She went in and stood for a minute or two looking at Fidelia but really facing some truths about herself. She had not given herself to Douglas as generously as a wife should. She had not been content with him as he was but had wanted him to change his nature to suit her. She had been like that when a child, to the exasperation of her playmates who were happy with themselves as they were. Did Angus want to paint her because he had seen in her face that witch-like discontent?

When Fidelia and Letty came, she must try not to interfere.

After breakfast she did what little housework was needed. Angus, she saw, was a more conscientious housekeeper than herself. Just the same she went round with the pink feather duster. She amused herself by imagining that today, 20th June, was when her husband, from the other world, paid his one visit of the year. His eyes were the colour of kelp, his hair yellow as withered marram grass. He would stay the night and they would make love. She would become pregnant. She would have a child, a girl, half-human and half-pixie.

You're at it again, Janet McDonald, she said sternly to herself in the mirror with the silver frame. Douglas is right. You're not grown up. If you're not careful, you'll go off your head like Auntie Chrissie. You've got a cheek making fun of Douglas because he wants a son who'll be able to break par before he's fourteen.

In spite of this self-reproof, when she went outside half an hour later and and saw that the bread had been removed from the scallop shell, she thought of demons, not birds.

Between half past eleven and twelve she kept expecting to hear the taxi arriving with Fidelia and Letty. By one she knew it was not coming today. It would come tomorrow.

After lunch she went out for a stroll about the house, wearing the red-and-black sarong and blouse. She soon got into the way of walking with the short steps enforced by the tightness of the skirt, and so was able to walk with Oriental elegance to meet the mail van. The postman, Donnie McMillan, middle-aged and an adherent of the Free Kirk, knew, as all Kildonan did, that Mr McNaught's cousin, a married woman, was living in sin with the artist McAllister. Here she was, brazen besom, swanking in an outlandish costume. He frowned at her as he handed her some letters. 'For Mr McAllister.' But to his cronies in the public bar that evening he was to say that she reminded him of the Queen of Sheba.

Most of the mail was the usual junk. There were two personal letters, one from stockbrokers in Glasgow, as it stated on the envelope. At the other she stared in astonishment. On the outside were the name and address of the sender: Mrs Nell

Ballantyne, 103 Orchard Road, Sydney, Australia. The stamp, though, was British and the postmark Diss, Norfolk.

Douglas, David, Mary, and Mr McPherson in her imagination gathered round and gasped in horrified disapproval as she sat on the step under the sheep's skull and tore open the letter from Nell. At least I'm not being deceitful, she told them. I could have steamed it open so that he would never know. As a matter of fact I'm doing it for his sake. This woman who's written to him, she's an Australian, I know about her, he might prefer not to hear from her. He might be grateful if he never saw this letter, if I just burned it. I can't tell until I've read it. He's in the throes of painting what he thinks will be his best picture ever and will make him famous. Naturally, he doesn't want to be interrupted or disturbed. It could mean him losing his inspiration. So, you see, I could be doing him a good turn by reading this letter.

It wasn't easy to read, so slapdash was the handwriting, and the language, she soon found, was shocking.

'Angus, you old Scotch bastard,

'This will be the third letter I've written you and not one fucking word in return. All those promises to defy the hordes of hell and come to my rescue and yet, when I write and tell you my heart's broken and I'm well and truly up shit creek, not a word to cheer me up. Nell's a tough lady, they all said, nothing and nobody could break Nell's heart, and she'd be a bloody fool to let a selfish cunt like Angus McAllister break it. That's what they all said, wasn't it, all those years ago? But you knew it wasn't true. You knew there were times when I was miserable. You tried to show it in that bloody awful painting you did of me.

'I expect you've got married and that's why you've never replied. I find it hard to believe. I'd got it into my head that you weren't the marrying kind. You put your painting first. I used to hate you for it. When I squeezed your balls, lover, I meant to hurt. Why I loved you I'll never know.

'I heard that after I'd gone you found consolation with a big

64

handsome dame from the Philippines, with sad eyes, but liable to stick a knife in you if you did the dirty on her. so my spies reported. But I believe you did the dirty on her too, and got away with it.

'Sorry, Angus, jealousy talking, I suppose. Desperation too. You used to tell me that when Bruce went back to Sydney he'd change his ways, he'd give up hitting golf balls and chasing slim chicks half his age. Well, you were wrong, sport. I admit the circumstances in which we did go back, flung out ignominiously was how they all saw it, because of my big mouth, weren't likely to make me precious to him again. Well, you might say, if you were to see me now, who would blame him? I've got a bit stouter than when you knew me. Statuesque, you called me then. Well, I'm more like an orang-utan now than when you made me look like one in that painting. Sorry again. I know you were proud of it and I used to think that, if that was how you saw me, what the hell, if it made you love me, and I still think that in your stingy Scotch way you did.

'You will have noticed, being an observant bugger, that I've just put Diss at the top of this letter. Deliberately. I'm in England visiting my sister Elsie who lives in this pleasant little town that's got a dignified old church where I go in and sit, and a small mere or lake where I feed the ducks. I've been trying to make up my mind whether I should pay you a visit while I'm here. Re-member you said that if I ever needed help I was to come to you, even if it was ten thousand miles, as Robbie Burns said. Well, it's not nearly as far as that and I certainly could do with some help. Elsie's afraid I'll drown myself in the mere. So I might if there weren't so many ducks. Today I went to a travel agent and I'm booked to fly from Glasgow to Flodday next Tuesday arriving at 11. If you've got married bring her along. We can still enjoy a drink and a chat for old times' sake. I promise to be very discreet. I can put up at a hotel and fly back in a day or two. I'd like to see your island hideaway. No harm done. Unless the woman you've married is the kind that can't forgive things that had damn-all to do with her. In which case, to hell with her.

'If I'd put my full address would you have sent a telegram telling me not to come?

Love.

Nell.'

10

There were no fences on the promontory, so that Charlie and his cows were free to roam all over it. They had favourite places for different times of the day. They always spent the night in the north-east corner, where, when the tide was out, it was possible to walk dry-shod across the sand to a small islet on which were the remains of a holy man's cell. The cattle had never been known to venture across. On warm days they liked to stand on the sand or in shallow water, but their noses seemed to tell them that the grass on their own machair was lusher and sweeter than that on the rocky islet. In this and other matters Charlie let himself be guided by his cows many of whom were older and wiser than himself. They took care of him. They knew what his purpose was among them and made it as convenient for him as they could, keeping out of the way when it wasn't their turn. If two were ready at the same time, one, usually the younger, stood by patiently. Sometimes, unable to control herself, she grew importunate. Charlie, his own patience exemplary, would turn aside and soothe her with a few loving licks. If some young stirk had the temerity, not to say the fond hope, to try to serve the cow Charlie was then courting, he would be pushed away with a gentle butt of the massive head. Charlie indeed seemed to have sympathy for those strong young bullocks whose manhood had been taken away. When all the cows capable of bearing young had been made pregnant – there were over 40 in Mr McCandlish's herds – Charlie, much thinner, was left on his own, his duty done. If he wanted to follow the herd, he was welcome. If he didn't, he could go and mope anywhere he wanted.

That morning he was on the shining sand with the cows. His copper ring glinted and the curls on top of his head were bright, as if he was wearing a crown: as indeed he should, being the king of all that domain. Rabbits, sheep, and birds all showed him deference. Yet, though magnificent, he was sad. All his progeny, as soon as they were big enough, were sold to the slaughter-house. To say that he did not know and therefore could not mind seemed to Angus unjust. The rheum that sometimes appeared in those big bloodshot eyes might or might not be tears, but Charlie in the autumn when he was alone had the melancholy dignity of a king all of whose sons were doomed.

Angus had always been keen to paint a vast picture celebrating his love of the promontory and its creatures. For that reason he had studied the ways of Charlie the king, who would be at the heart of it. It would also be a lament for all the beautiful and innocent creatures that had loved this place where they had been born: and also for the people forced to leave. His mother had taken him to visit Ardnave when he was about seven. She had been particularly delighted by the profusion of little blue but-terflies. Little blue butterflies would be in his picture.

When he had looked up and seen Charlie glaring down at him and Janet yesterday, the big white face had seemed curiously human. That had been the inspiration. In the painting he would give Charlie a human face. At first he had thought of using his own as a model, but he knew now that Douglas's would be more suitable. There was something bull-like in Douglas's face: the broadness of the brow, not signifying powerful intellect; the strong nose, adapted for lordly snorts: and above all, over the whole countenance, an assurance such as a king might have, a king, however, easily taken advantage of by cleverer men.

Charlie's body with Douglas's face would make a more evocative combination than the centaur. Janet's face could be given to the cow whose turn was next. She looked more intelligent than Douglas but then cows were more intelligent than bulls. That was the reason why they were never used in a bull-ring. Bulls kept attacking the red cape. Cows would soon realise that the attack should be made on the holder of the cape. If this was done, all that pirouetting and all those fancy skips would be of no avail to the matador.

He would not attempt to paint the bodies meticulously. It would be enough to convey in the one case strength, vigour, and potency, and in the other femininity and beauty.

He walked down on to the sand and stood among the cows with his sketch-book in his hand. Charlie, aware of his presence, turned his head, peered at him – according to Mr McCandlish bulls had poor eyesight – swished his tail and went back to dreaming. A small bird landed on his back; sandflies leapt up and annoyed his legs: sea-going flies from the cowpats on the machair buzzed round his eyes: he paid them all no heed. His patience and amiability were admirable. He was enjoying this spell of off-duty.

One of the cows at last began to wander off towards the machair. Others followed, one by one, in leisurely fashion. As they passed Angus, they glanced at him with curiosity but without animosity. They did not know what he was doing there but whatever it was it was his business. Each weighed several hundredweight. If one had crashed into him he might have been seriously hurt. None did, though two or three young stirks pranced round him playfully.

When all the cows were back on the grass grazing, Charlie remained on the sand, still in a dwam. Terns dived close to his head, gulls made a clamour above him: it was as if they were trying to warn him that the tide was coming in fast. One of the cows, perhaps with the same purpose, lowed persistently.

At last, with the water up to his houghs, he came ashore, and at once resumed his duties, going from one cow to another sniffing at each, and then raising his head as if to savour what he had just sniffed, like a vineyard owner testing his wine. There was none in the right condition, so, with what looked like a shrug of relief, he began grazing like the rest.

Angus sat on a bank amongst them and sketched undisturbed.

About 11 o'clock he heard and saw, in the distance, the daily plane from Glasgow, coming down to land at Flodday air-field. According to Janet the witch, Fidelia and Letty might be on board. He could think of nothing less likely to be true. Letty would be ten now, better able than ever to dominate her mother. For years she had urged her mother to go home to the Philippines. Perhaps they were already there. Letty could well be the means of re-uniting her parents. She was beautiful, clever, and astute enough.

He had said goodbye to Fidelia at Basah airport with sorrow, but also with relief, which he had kept hidden. He would never understand how he had found the courage to be her lover. It had needed duplicity too, but that had been easy to find. People had sneered at him behind his back and sometimes to his face. He had never been brave in confronting prejudice. Little Letty, more percipient than her mother or rather not blinded by love, had seen through him.

Mr Amaladoss, a white-haired Tamil on the College staff, had once whispered into his ear: 'Mrs Gomez is a very beautiful lady, Mr McAllister, with a sweet nature, and we all love her, but do not forget that all of her ancestors were not, like yours and mine, civilised persons. She has the blood of headhunters in her, you see.'

Though what Amaladoss had said was malicious nonsense, she and Letty would have been out of place on Flodday.

About half past three, with a bookful of successful sketches, he set off for home.

70

11

He was surprised and displeased when he came in sight of the house and saw that his car had gone. He should have hidden the keys. When he took the sketches into the studio, he noticed that the portrait of Nell was on the easel. He promptly put it back among the paintings stacked against the wall. Janet would have to be told to leave things alone.

In the living-room he found, Sellotaped to Buddha's brow, a message from her: 'Borrowed the car to go into Kildonan for a few things. The cupboard's bare. Janet.' Whose money was she using, he wondered, and looked in the drawer where he kept his wallet. It was still there, with none of its contents missing. He always knew how much money he had. He had to be careful, for it had been some time since he had sold a picture. The last two he had sent to the gallery had been returned. He depended on his investments. He always waited anxiously for his stockbrokers' monthly reports. He expected this month's any day now.

Upstairs he discovered his guest's impudent activities. In one of the bedrooms she had spread out sheets and blankets to air. So she was keeping up her lunatic belief that Fidelia and Letty were coming. Her claiming to have second sight was annoying, but tolerable if treated as a joke. Her acting as if her prophecies were going to come true was insupportable. No wonder her husband had skelped her.

Reminded, he went to her room to have another long look at Douglas in the photograph. He had had some doubts as to whether giving the bull a human face was an idea that would work. Now he was confident that it would, if the face was Douglas's.

He was in his studio making sketches from the photograph when he heard the car. He rushed upstairs and replaced the photograph by her bedside.

He cringed when he went down and found her carrying in a number of parcels, but he had to pretend to be pleased. He had let her see that he was physically timid, he must not let her see that he was also parsimonious. When she produced a bottle of wine and announced proudly that it had cost nearly ten pounds he groaned, but inwardly. He himself never bought any that cost as much as that. Among other things, she had bought fresh salmon, avocados, and asparagus, which were dear anywhere but on the island exorbitant.

'Don't worry,' she said. 'It was my own money.'

'You shouldn't. You're my guest. If you tell me how much it all cost, I'll pay you back.'

'Twenty-nine pounds and fifty-seven pence. But I'm not really a guest, am I? I'm a lodger. Consider this is in lieu of rent. By the way, your mail came. Mostly junk. But a letter from stockbrokers.'

He was eager to see it. It was not likely he would be able to keep himself by his painting for some time yet, if ever. His investments were important. A glance reassured him. Substantial profits were reported. The cheque enclosed was for a bigger amount than he had expected.

It did not occur to him to ask if there had been any other letter. He so seldom received any.

She was busy in the kitchen. 'Guess who I bumped into,' she called.

'Your cousin?'

'No. Mr McPherson. He said he's coming out to see you.'

'What for?'

'I think to threaten you with hell-fire for seducing a married woman.'

72

'I hope you told him I have not seduced you and have no intention of doing so.'

She laughed. 'I tried to but he didn't believe me. I suppose it's more interesting for him if people are wicked. Did you get a lot of sketching done?'

'Yes, I did.'

That was a reminder that there was work waiting for him in the studio.

He was still hard at it when she knocked at the door about two hours later. He had taken the precaution of locking it. From now on nobody would be allowed to see his painting until it was finished.

'Dinner will be ready in half an hour,' she said.

'Thank you.' He felt beneficent not only towards her but towards the whole world. The painting was taking shape and going well.

'You could have a shower,' she said. 'I've had one. The water's still warm. I think there should be enough.'

He smiled. She was a child, concerned about trifles. They were all childish. Only the artist was truly mature.

Though it was still broad daylight, she had candles on the table. His best napery, cutlery, and delf were in use. His pewter vase from Selangor was filled with wild flowers. She herself was comely in a sleeveless red dress. Fixed to her hair was the golden scorpion he had bought in Phnom Penh. He refrained from remarking how appropriate an emblem it was. He was still feeling beneficent.

She had boasted that she was a good cook and the meal proved it. The wine, now that he knew she had paid for it, was excellent, and he had the whole bottle to himself. She drank orange juice. She kept giving him looks that, if he had not been feeling compassionate, he would have called sly. He called them wistful. He almost teased her about getting the bedroom ready for mythical visitors, but his compassion fell short of that.

They went into the living-room to drink their coffee. He sat on the red divan, she on the green. Buddha smiled on them.

'Was it good news from your stockbroker?' she asked.

'Very good news.'

'Douglas has got a lot of shares in Glaxo.'

'So have I. A most efficient company. May I congratulate you on a delicious meal?'

'Thanks. I'm glad you enjoyed it. You see, I've got something to tell you that may come as a bit of a shock.'

He chuckled. 'Are you thinking of leaving before Saturday? Has Mr McPherson put the fear of God into you?'

'You got another letter today.'

'Did I indeed? Where is it, may I ask?'

'Perhaps you won't want to read it when I tell you who it's from.'

He frowned. Surely it couldn't be from Fidelia?

'It's from Mrs Ballantyne. Nell.'

He felt relieved. 'Oh, Nell. She's written before. A most profane correspondent.'

'She certainly is. I've read it.'

What with the wine, beneficence, and compassion, he had difficulty in finding the right reaction. 'You've read it?'

'Her name was on the envelope. I know that all you want is to get on with your painting undisturbed. So I thought I'd better read it first.'

'How could you read it? Was the envelope not sealed?'

'I tore it open. I could have steamed it open but that would have been dishonest.'

'You mean to say you opened and read my letter without permission?'

'In a way, I did ask your permission. Psychically. Didn't you hear my voice when you were on the machair?'

'Do you know what you are, Mrs Maxwell? You're a damned

74

impudent interfering sly bitch. Don't you know it's a criminal offence to open another person's mail?'

'The M15 do it all the time.'

That was a joke. He didn't find it amusing but it put him off his stride.

'You're going to need my help, Angus, so it would be silly to fall out with me. Nell's coming to Flodday. Tomorrow, yes, tomorrow. She's flying from Glasgow. I thought you might not want to see her. She sounds a vulgar coarse woman. I got out that picture you painted of her for another look. If you don't want her to come here, I could easily prevent her by pretending to be your wife. She says in the letter that, if you're married, then she'll just go away again.'

All this was too much for him. The wine's effect was growing stronger, and the dregs of beneficence and compassion were clouding his mind. 'Where is the letter?'

She got up and took it from between the pages of the book of erotic sculptures.

He thought, wildly, that Nell's bosom and bottom would have qualified her for an apsaras, but not her waist.

He read the letter and was surprised that his compassion revived, this time for Nell. It was not like her to feel sorry for herself. He also felt sexually roused, as he remembered that big soft hospitable body. After all, his present state of mind, edgy with creativeness, was akin to sexual desire. But she must not come to Ardnave. Janet the witch was right. His inspiration would wither and die.

'What does she mean,' asked Janet, 'by saying that her big mouth got them flung out?'

'She told an influential Malay politician to his face that he was a dirty little crook.'

'*Was* he a dirty little crook?'

Little, because he was only five foot high; a crook, because he had used his position to award himself a timber concession worth millions of dollars: and dirty, because he had got two white expatriate women to sleep with him in return for promising their husbands a renewal of contract, with improved conditions.

'Most people thought so.' Most people had also thought that Nell should have held her tongue. She had not done the white expatriate cause any good.

'But she was the only one with the courage to tell him so. Good for her. What age is she?'

'I don't know. About forty-four.'

'And fatter than ever, as she says herself. Well, do you want her to come to Ardnave?'

He shook his head.

'Then do you want me to meet her and tell her I'm your wife?'

'You'd have to do it very convincingly. She's not easily taken in.'

'Don't worry. I'm a good actress. I'll wear my wedding ring. She's half expecting to meet your wife. She says so. So why shouldn't she believe me?'

'She might think that you're not the kind of woman I would have married.'

'What kind of woman's that, for heaven's sake?'

'Do you think I should go with you to meet her?'

'No. You wouldn't be able to keep it up. I'll tell her you're too busy with your painting, which happens to be true. No woman with pride will go where she's not wanted.'

He was too dispirited to jeer.

'It's different with me. I'm leaving on Saturday. She might want to stay for months or years. I don't want to sleep with you. She might.'

What was worse, he might want to sleep with Nell. Let that happen and he was doomed as a painter. He had once accused her of being a succubus. Unfortunately he had had to explain

76

what it meant: the effect had been spoiled. She had laughed heartily and been more succubine than ever.

How much happier and more creative he had felt on the machair with Charlie and his cows. Women brought too many complications.

12

Janet dressed smartly in a skirt of McDonald tartan, a white blouse and a lemon-coloured cardigan. She did not want to let Angus down.

'Have you any message for her?' she asked.

He mumbled. 'Just say I'm very sorry but I know she'll understand.'

'She won't but I'll tell her anyway. I'm sure I'll recognise her. Well, cheerio.'

This was the kind of adventure she liked. She was the heroine, Nell the villainess. Angus would have to do as the hero.

As she drove towards the airport she considered what she should do if Fidelia and Letty were also on the plane. It would be an awkward situation but she was sure she could cope. Angus, however, might have to be recast as the villain.

When she arrived at the airport, which consisted of a big tin shed, a Land-Rover was chasing sheep off the runway. The windsocks were limp. The sun shone. There would be a safe landing for the passengers whatever other misfortunes lay in store for them.

People were waiting to greet arrivals or to board the plane on its return trip. Most of them were Kildonan natives who knew that she was Mr McNaught's cousin who was living in sin out at Ardnave with McAllister the painter. One or two of the men grinned lecherously, as if wishing she had chosen them instead of a shilpit creature like McAllister. The women frowned, as if to demand why they should have to stay at home like hens while she was free as a swan. One woman approached her. To her dismay, she saw that it was Mrs McPherson, the minister's wife, grim-faced and dumpy, wearing a hairy green tweed costume and a hat like a chamberpot. Prepared for abuse or even a contemptuous slap, Janet was taken a back when the older woman smiled and said: 'It must be paradise at Ardnave in weather like this.' Without waiting for an answer she went back to her friends, low-heeled and stumpy-legged.

Janet was amazed. She had always thought of Mrs McPherson as puritanic and narrow-minded like her husband.

There was a roar overhead as the plane came in to land. Everybody took up position to watch the passengers come down the steps.

Janet recognised at once the big woman in the green coat as Mrs Ballantyne, but she looked in vain for Fidelia and Letty. There was no dark-faced woman with a little girl.

She went over and addressed Mrs Ballantyne. 'Good morning,' she said. 'Are you Mrs Ballantyne?'

Tired, rather sad, but shrewd, light blue eyes regarded her. 'That's my name. What's yours?'

'I'm Angus's wife.'

'Is that so? So you're the reason the bastard has never written?'

Janet smiled warily. She had expected Nell to be fatter. Douglas would have called her a fine figure of a woman.

'Where is he?' asked Nell, looking about.

'He couldn't come.'

'Why, has he broken a leg?'

'He's very busy with a new painting. He thinks it's going to be his masterpiece.'

'Doesn't he think that about them all? He used to, anyway.'

'To tell you the truth, Mrs Ballantyne, he thought that when you knew he was married you wouldn't want to see him.'

'Bullshit. I said in my letter that if he was married to bring his wife with him and we'd have a drink together.'

If Janet had taken a dislike to the big Australian it would have been easy to assume haughtiness and defend Angus, but instead she liked her and was ashamed of deceiving her.

'Well, it doesn't matter,' said Nell. 'I think it was the island itself I wanted to see. It looked lovely from the plane. He used to talk a lot about it. Peace and quiet, he said. As I said in my letter, I'll move into a hotel for a day or two and then go back. No harm done.'

'Go back to Diss, do you mean?'

'No, to Sydney. I've brought all my stuff with me. I've said my goodbyes to Elsie.'

By this time the luggage had been brought into the shed. Nell pointed out hers, with QANTAS labels attached. She carried one and Janet the other to the car.

'I'm on slippery ground,' she said, 'but what kind of husband does he make? You see, I never thought he would ever marry. I would have bet money on it. Too bloody selfish, I used to tell him.'

'He puts his painting before everything else.'

'He always did. How long have you been married?'

It was then that Janet blundered. 'Five years,' she said. That was how long she had been married to Douglas.

They were at the car, lifting the suitcases into the boot. Nell looked puzzled.

'Didn't he leave Basah just three years ago? You couldn't have got married there. I don't remember you ever being mentioned.'

Mrs McPherson passed them. 'Good morning, Mrs Maxwell,' she said. 'Be sure and give my regards to Mr McAllister.'

Disconcerted by that inexplicable cordiality, Janet was at a loss when Nell asked why the lady had addressed her as Mrs Maxwell.

They got into the car.

'What did she mean?' asked Nell.

'She made a mistake, that's all.'

81

'A woman that'd wear a hat like that never makes a mistake. What's your game, Mrs Maxwell?'

'I don't know what you mean.'

'You're not Angus's wife. For one thing he'll never get married, and for another he wouldn't marry a dame like you. That's a compliment by the way. You look too tricky for him. Who the hell are you then?'

Janet decided the game was up. Besides, it would be more interesting with Nell at Ardnave. 'You're quite right. My name *is* Mrs Maxwell. At present I'm staying with Angus at Ardnave.'

'You his girlfriend? That's more like him. He's always preferred women who were already married. Is there a Mr Maxwell?'

'Yes.'

'Does he live here on the island?'

'No, in Glasgow.'

'You're separated then? Is that it?'

'Not really. He's coming on Saturday for me. I ought to make it clear that I'm just a lodger at Ardnave. I don't sleep with Angus. I met him for the first time last Saturday, just four days ago.'

'How did you come to be his lodger?'

'I invited myself.'

'Yes, I can see you would. He'd love that, I don't think. You met him last Saturday. When did you move in?'

'On Sunday.'

Nell laughed. 'You're a cool one, Mrs Maxwell. What's your first name?'

'Janet.'

'Mine's Nell. May I ask why you left Mr Maxwell in Glasgow?'

They were now approaching Kildonan.

Janet might tell her later but not now. 'Let's just say he's too fond of golf. Like your husband, I believe.'

82

'You believe right. Is there any place here where I could send a cable?'

'The post office, I suppose.'

'Would you stop there, please?'

Janet stopped the car outside the post office. She got out too, intending to go into the post office with Nell. She wanted to find out to whom the cable was being sent.

'I'll manage on my own,' said Nell, brusquely. 'They speak English, don't they?'

Janet waited outside. People passing gave her inquisitive stares. She stared back haughtily.

About five minutes later Nell reappeared. 'They were speaking a foreign language in there.'

'But you managed all right? It would be Gaelic.'

'Thanks.' Nell was looking at the little harbour, with yachts anchored in it. 'I like this place. As he said, peace and quiet. Well, Janet, I can see you're like me, a nosy bitch. The cable was to Bruce, my husband. I've come all those thousands of miles to get out of his way, and I'm waiting for him to come round that corner. If he did, I don't suppose he'd give me a second look but me, I'd weep with joy. I said I would be away for five months but it's only been two and I've sent a cable to say I'll be back some time next week.'

If Douglas came round that corner, thought Janet, I'd be pleased to see him but I would have to tell him he's come too soon. In the drama that's going to take place at Ardnave in the next two or three days there's no role for him.

It was Mr McPherson the minister who came round the corner, black from hat to elastic-sided boots. He carried a shopping bag. He stopped beside them. There was a smell of mothballs off him.

'Good day, Mrs Maxwell,' he said, showing yellow teeth. 'I trust that you have given up sinful ways and have now returned to the flock of the godly.' Then he walked on, with a curious swagger.

'What sinful ways?' asked Nell, laughing.

'They all think that because I'm staying with Angus I must be sleeping with him. Probably you think it too.'

'Not me. You said you invited yourself. I know what Angus thinks of pushy ladies. Though, mind you, I am interested to find out what your relationship with him is. Now what are we going to do? Shall we go for a drink before we go out to this place Ardnave. Though it'd have to be tea or coffee or orange juice for me. I'm on the wagon. I used to be a fat slob, to tell the truth. So I'm trying to lose weight. I'm wearing a girdle to hold in my guts and it's murder.'

'I think we should go straight out to Ardnave after I've done some shopping. I've to pick up two canisters of gas. There's no electricity at Ardnave.'

'I think I should take a bottle to Angus. They make whisky here, don't they? A bottle of the local stuff then. Any suggestions?'

'I never drink whisky myself but they say Flodday Mist is the best.'

13

Never had his brain seethed with so many ideas, never had his hand shown such swift skill. This painting was going to be the biggest in size and the most ambitious in theme. The canvas covered a whole wall. He would have to stand on steps to paint the sky. In the past his problem had been to conceive a painting as an organic whole and not a number of sections which, however well executed, remained inertly separate. It was going to be very different with 'Taurus', as he provisionally called it. In his imagination it was already complete and perfect to the last violet. Often before the beauty and originality of the vision in his mind had come out in paint as dull and conventional. Not this time. It wasn't spurious second sight like Janet's but artistic instinct which whispered to him that this painting would be a masterpiece. He would have joined the immortals. It behoved him therefore to think kindly of all those not similarly exalted, such as Janet and Nell.

He did not, however, devote much thought to them that morning. He was too engrossed in his work. One of his sketches of Charlie particularly pleased him. It was of the big bull sniffing the air deliciously in the mysterious act of gauging whether the cow beside him was ready for conception. All the magic of creation was contained in those sniffs. To that drawing he added a face as like Douglas's as he could make it. The result astonished him. It was the first of many surprises that this painting would give him, its creator. Some uncanny force was guiding his hand. At the centre would be the man-bull, emanating mysteries of its

85

own. Had not the ancient Cretans adorned their statues of the goddess Artemis with garlands of bulls' testicles, carved in marble?

He did not notice the arrival of the car nor the women's voices outside.

A banging on the door jolted him back to his ordinary senses. A woman's voice behind it shouted: 'What kind of welcome's this, you rude bugger?'

Annoyance at being interrupted was swept out of his mind by benignity that embraced not only Nell and Janet, nuisances though they were, but everyone, including their absurd husbands.

He did not merely shake Nell's hand or give her a chaste kiss on the cheek, but threw his arms about her and kissed her on the mouth passionately, to her own amusement and Janet's indignation.

What cheek, said Janet's Free Kirk face, sending me to the airport to tell this woman that I was your wife so that she would go away and not bother you, and now here you are kissing her as if she was your long-lost love.

His artist's mind, never more alert, took note, and also of Nell's sudden tears.

Poor Nell was not to know that he had not really kissed her but rather whatever goddess it was that inspired painters.

'I ought to warn you, Angus,' she said, 'before you get any ideas. I've just sent a cable to Bruce telling him to expect me home some time next week. So I'll only be here for a few days.'

'That's splendid, Nell. I mean about you and Bruce. Nothing would make me happier than to know that you and he were reconciled again.'

Nell laughed. 'Liar.'

She kept reminding Janet of someone. She soon discovered who when she saw how Nell, simply by being there, took all the magic out of things. She had done it with the sheep's skull and the mask of the demon, and now in the living-room she was doing it with the dragon on the ceiling and Buddha. Douglas too would have dismissed them all as grotesque objects in bad taste.

'I see you brought Bud back with you,' said Nell. 'God knows why. He's never brought you blessings, has he? But then, how could he, considering how you got him.' She turned to Janet. 'It was pinched from a temple somewhere in Indonesia. I used to tell him it would bring bad luck, not good.'

Janet remembered her presentiment about that room. She did not mention it, just as she had not mentioned the coming of Fidelia. Nell was too crude an unbeliever.

Meanwhile, need to get back to his painting had been mounting in Angus unbearably. 'I hope you don't mind, ladies, but there's something I must see to. Janet, would you please make Nell at home? I should be free for lunch in about an hour. We'll have a long talk then, Nell.'

'Aren't you going to help carry her cases upstairs?' asked Janet, crossly.

'We can manage ourselves,' said Nell. 'Go and add a daub or two, Angus. We'll be delighted to see you at lunch. We bought some prime Scotch steak and a bottle of the local beverage, Flodday Mist. You'll have to drink it all yourself. I'm on the wagon. Not even wine or beer. I don't eat like a pig any more. I'm trying to make myself beautiful again. But not for you, sport.'

'You were always beautiful for me, Nell.'

'Bullshit.'

Upstairs in her room Nell took off her girdle. It was a difficult and, to Janet, immodest operation. Stripped to bra and knickers, she sat on the bed and, with groans, rolled down the tight elastic inch by inch. Slowly her stomach escaped, white and flabby and marked with the pattern of the girdle. It was not a pretty sight, especially as tufts of red hair were also exposed. 'Thank Christ for that,' she said, as she lay back on the bed, puffing and panting with relief.

Janet was finding Nell too much for her. She could put up with her bad language and lack of modesty, but not her lack of reverence. Buddha might be a heathen god, but millions of people believed in him, so he ought not to have been called Bud, as if he was a taxi-driver.

'I could do with a fag,' said Nell, 'but I've given them up too. A bloody paragon, that's me. Sit down and tell me why you ran away from your man.'

Janet sat on the only chair. She saw in the dressing-table mirror that she had her lips pursed in a way that Mr McPherson would have approved. She tried to smile. 'He hit me,' she said.

'I hope you hit him back.'

'I did.'

'Good on you. Was it the first time or did he make a habit of it?'

'It was the first time.'

'Tell me about it. It always helps to spill it out.'

'I went to Skye to visit my parents.'

'Skye? That's a famous island, isn't it? There's a song about it. Bruce used to sing it. His grandparents were Scotch, you know.'

'I came home a day before I was expected. I found him and a woman practising putting on the sitting-room carpet.'

'Well, where was the harm in that?'

'They had no clothes on.'

Nell laughed. 'Maybe it was a heat wave. It's unlikely, I admit, but maybe that was all they were doing, practising putting. He's a keen golfer, you said.'

'They looked guilty.'

'I bet.'

'He had the cheek to blame me for coming home a day too soon. So I picked up a putter and hit him.'

'Well done. Did you hit her too?'

'No. I didn't care about her. I don't think she was the first.'

'If you hit him hard enough she might be the last. So you decided to come to Flodday and let him stew for a while?'

'Yes. My cousin's wife owns a hotel here.'

'If you'll pardon me saying so, Janet, you're giving me the impression that sex is a very serious matter to you.'

'So it is. So it should be.'

'Sure. But it should be fun too, you know.'

'Fun? Isn't it supposed to be a kind of sacrament?'

'Hell, yes, but that doesn't mean it can't be fun.'

'If it's not a sacrament, then it's just a thing that animals do.'

'Well, what's wrong with that? Animals take it very seriously. For them it's more of a sacrament than it is for us. It has to be. It can't be anything else. Nature sees to that. Continuation of the species. You didn't say if you had any kids yourself.'

'Not yet. Douglas doesn't want any till he's thirty.'

'You mean, while his handicap is still low. When will he be thirty?'

'This November.'

Nell laughed at what she evidently considered Scotch caution. 'I've got two. Bruce junior, he's twenty-two. Madge is nineteen. I love them but they've given me some sore hearts. Drugs and sex. To be fair, maybe I've not shown them a very good example. It's going to be different when I get back. Would you like to see some photographs? Pass me that handbag, please.'

Janet fetched the handbag and Nell took from it some photographs.

There was one of her daughter, a red-haired freckled girl with a stubborn jaw, very like her mother. One of her son, long-haired, with a shy friendly grin. One of the whole family when the children were small, with Sydney Harbour Bridge in the background.

'Here's one you might find disgusting,' said Nell. 'Me, I think it's beautiful. I took it with a Polaroid on our honeymoon.'

89

It was of her husband Bruce, stark-naked, striking a pose to show off his muscles. His private parts were not concealed.

Janet was in a quandary. She did find the photograph disgusting but she had often wished that she had one of Douglas in the same state.

'He took one of me,' said Nell. 'I was worth looking at then in the buff. I didn't have this.' She slapped her stomach. 'Mind you, he's put on a lot of weight himself since.'

'Why didn't he come with you?' asked Janet.

'Hell, I was running away from him. I made the excuse that I wanted to see my sister Elsie.

'Did he mind you going?'

'What do you think? He was glad to get rid of me. I wouldn't be surprised if by the time I go home next week he'd started proceedings for a divorce.'

'Would you agree to a divorce?'

'I'd have to, wouldn't I? What's the good of living with a man who doesn't want you? Well, shall we go down and give our host his lunch? To tell the truth, I'm hungry myself. I don't eat enough nowadays, trying to lose weight.'

'All right. I'll go and get things started while you get dressed.'

As Janet passed Angus's bedroom, she saw to it that the door was closed. She didn't want Nell to see the painting of Fidelia, at least not yet. She was beginning to resent Nell's presence there, not for her own sake but for Fidelia's.

14

Though Janet did most of the cooking, and of the serving too, the two others, eagerly reminiscing about Basah, paid her as little heed as they would have done if she had been a waitress. Not usually patient under slights, she bided her time.

They were discussing 'the dirty little crook'.

'What happened to him?' asked Nell. 'I heard he's been kicked out himself.'

'Nobody really knew. Politics were very secret there as well as corrupt. But whether he was kicked out or left of his own accord, he certainly took his ill-gotten riches with him. So he's probably in Barbados or some such sybaritic spot, living in a five-star hotel with a golf course handy.'

'Yes, he was fond of golf, wasn't he?'

'I believe those who played with the Tun had to let him win.'

'Bruce would never have done that. Golf was a religion to him. It still is. He was a bit of a randy goat, the Tun I mean. He liked white women best. I could tell you stories. I bet in that five-star hotel he's got a bevy of them.'

While they chatted, Janet attended to them in silence. It cost her a great effort. She did not mind Angus so much, it was his house after all, but the gall of Nell, a newcomer, made her choke. She felt sympathy for Bruce. No doubt he had made golf his religion because his wife had failed him. But could that not be said about Douglas and her? She shuddered, but the others did not notice.

For over an hour they went on discussing people Janet had never heard of. It was the height of rudeness.

It came to a sudden end when Angus jumped to his feet and rushed out, bound not for the bathroom upstairs, as Nell facetiously suggested, but for his studio.

'So that's how genius strikes?' said Nell. 'Like diarrhoea.' She laughed coarsely.

Janet collected the dishes to carry them into the kitchen.

'I'll wash,' she said. 'You can dry.'

'I'm not much of a housewife,' said Nell, getting up. 'I usually let the dishes pile up. Bruce didn't like it.'

She was wearing green Bermuda shorts and looked ridiculous. Without the girdle her stomach stuck out.

They were in the kitchen when they heard the tooting of a motor horn. Janet looked out of the window and saw the red mail van.

She hurried out. The postman looked disappointed when he saw that she was wearing Western dress. Like all Kildonan by this time, he had heard that another woman, an Australian by her accent, had joined McAllister's menage. He had hoped to be able to take back a report to the public bar that evening.

'Anything for me?' called Nell. 'Elsie said she would send anything on.'

Janet sat down in the living-room, with the letter in her hand. 'No. Just one for Angus. It's got a foreign stamp. A bird in a tree with red flowers.'

Nell come in from the kitchen, with a towel in her hand. 'Hibiscus,' she said. 'That's a Basah stamp. Who still writes to him from there?'

'We'll soon find out,' said Janet, and she tore open the envelope.

Nell was shocked. 'What the hell are you doing? That's Angus's letter. It's private. Did he say you could open his letters?'

'I have my reasons.' Janet meant that it might be from Fidelia.

'Reasons? What are you talking about? I said you were a nosy

92

bitch like me, but you're worse than I ever was. Even I wouldn't open Bruce's letters. I've a good mind to go and tell Angus.'

'It's from someone called Patel, a lawyer.'

'I know him. An Indian, black as coal, a creep, always grinning. If you kicked him in the teeth he'd still go on grinning. Nobody trusted him. What the hell's he writing to Angus for?'

'Do you really want to know? Shall I read it out?'

'All right, since you've opened it. But I'm going to tell Angus I had nothing to do with it.'

'Please yourself.'

Janet then read it out.

'Dear Mr McAllister,

'I write on behalf of my client, Mrs Fidelia Gomez. It is most probable that she has embarked on a course of action, advised against by myself, which could emerge to her detriment and could implicate your worthy self. For some time I have been negotiating on her behalf, without avail, I regret to say. A lawyer representing Mr Gomez of Manila arrived in Basah with two court orders, one issued in the Philippines and the other in Malaysia, awarding him custody of the child Letitia Gomez. We appealed against these iniquitous orders, without success. As you know, this is a Moslem country, where women do not enjoy the same rights as in my own native land or in yours. All was done that could legally be done. In the end I had no alternative but to advise Mrs Gomez to surrender the child. Yesterday I learned that she had quitted Basah, en route to Singapore and, it could well be, to the UK. She often spoke of you as someone in that country who would vouch for her. Sir, it is evidently her intention to plead with you to help her flout the law. Common humanity will persuade you to do so, common sense and my sincere advice counsel otherwise. The unfortunate lady is in effect a fugitive from justice. Her husband is a wealthy man able to afford skilful and cunning lawyers. You could find yourself under threat of prosecution if you were to allow pity to guide you. If she appears on your doorstep, you must urge her to return forthwith to Basah with the child. We would then continue the fight. I have already had a visit from the lawyer acting for Mr Gomez. He more or less accused me of collusion in her flight and demanded that I inform him of her present whereabouts. I told him nothing, but there are in this town numerous sources, former acquaintances of yours, who, it seems, were only too willing to sell him the relevant information.

'When you were in Basah, sir, our paths did not cross. It may interest you to know that I once bought a painting done by you. It is the head of a Dusun woman wearing a blue-and-pink head-dress. It adorns my home and is much admired. May I offer you my best wishes?

Yours sincerely

P.V. Patel.'

There was silence in the living-room. Outside oystercatchers flew past, piping shrilly. A sheep bleated.

'Well, I've got to say it,' said Nell. 'She'd have a damned nerve coming here. We're sorry for her, sure, but why should she bother Angus with her troubles?'

'He told her that if she ever needed help she should come to him.'

'She should have had the savvy to know he didn't mean it. How could he mean it? He had his life to lead here, she had hers to lead there. Everybody makes promises of that kind. They don't expect to be held to them. This kid, how old is she?'

'About ten.'

'I wonder what *she* thinks about it. Maybe, for all we know, she wants to be with her father, especially if he's really rich and lives in Forbes Park. That's an area of Manila where the cheapest house costs two million dollars. Armed guards are on duty day and night.'

'Gomez owns brothels and night-clubs.'

'I know his type. I was in Manila once. They sit beside you in the cinema. There's a notice at the box office requesting clients to check in their guns. They don't, so you're sitting there enjoying *The Sound of Music*, surrounded by sweet-smelling gents fingering their guns and pricks.'

Fidelia might have the blood of headhunters in her, thought Janet, but she was more of a lady than Nell would ever be.

'You're not taking into consideration,' she said, 'that Angus was in love with her once. I think he still is, if he would only admit it.'

'Bullshit. He never was in love with any woman, except his mother, and that's different. When he got drunk, which wasn't often, he used to talk about her and cry. I believe she's buried on the island.'

'If you want to see proof that he loved Fidelia, come with me.'

Nell followed up the stairs. 'If you're going to show me letters she wrote, it won't do. I'm ready to believe that she might have thought he was in love with her, but that doesn't mean he was.'

Janet opened the door. 'Wasn't that painted by a man in love?'

Nell sat on the bed and stared at the painting. 'By a man that loved her body, I'll give you that. Which is not quite the same. Don't forget he's an artist. He used to paint little Chinese whores. You'd have said he loved them, if you'd seen those paintings. He painted me once.'

'I've seen it.'

'I used to tell him he'd made me look like an orang-utan begging for a banana. But I didn't mean it. I like to put on an act of being tough. I'm good at it. I've noticed you wincing once or twice. But at heart I'm soft. I'm easily hurt, though you wouldn't think so to look at me. Well, you can see it plainly in that painting. So I guess it must be good, if it's truthful. Maybe he's a better artist than I've given him credit for. I know damn-all about art, so maybe I shouldn't have an opinion. This one he's working on now, what's it about?'

'He hasn't said and I've never seen it. He keeps the door locked. Let's go to your room. I want to talk to you about the letter.'

In her room Nell lay on the bed and Janet sat on the chair.

'Couldn't you patch up the envelope somehow?' asked Nell. 'So that he wouldn't know it had been opened?'

'That would be dishonest.'

'Dishonest? What the hell do you call opening somebody else's letters?'

'When Fidelia comes, we must make sure that he's fair to her.'

'Why should we? We've got no right to interfere. It's none of our business. Anyway, she won't come. Patel was just trying to show how smart he is. He's got no idea where she's gone. She could be in Manila, for all he knows.'

'She's coming here.'

Nell spoke irritably. 'What makes you so sure?'

'Because I have seen her and her little girl out there in front of the house. I have second sight, you see. It's been in my family for generations.'

'Is that so?' Nell was more flabbergasted than incredulous.

'I saw them as clearly as I'm seeing you now. Fidelia was wearing a blue coat and white skirt, Letitia a white coat and red dress. She had a ribbon in her hair and she was carrying a doll.'

'You saw all that?'

'Yes.'

'It's easy to make up a tale like that, when you know there's no chance of it ever being disproved.'

'When they come, you'll see it's all true.'

'And when is that?'

'Tomorrow, or the day after. Very soon.'

Nell sighed. 'Janet, would you please go away. You've got my head spinning. I'm not going to argue with you. If they step off the plane tomorrow or the day after, one of them wearing a blue coat and the other a white coat, I'll crown you queen of the witches.'

15

Janet waited till after dinner before telling Angus that a letter had come for him.

Angus was in a euphoric, benevolent mood. The painting was still going well. The demons were safely appeased.

'Yes, I thought I heard the postman. Bumf, I suppose. Where is it?'

'She opened it and read it,' said Nell. 'I had nothing to do with it. I told her she shouldn't.'

He smiled. He felt like a man who had just been told that he had won half-a-million pounds on the football pools. His benevolence was all-embracing. In any case, the letter was probably an appeal from some charity.

'Is this a disease you have, Janet, opening other people's mail?'

'It's from Basah. A lawyer called Patel.'

'You remember him, Angus,' said Nell. 'An Indian. He was always trying to join the yacht club. They always black-balled him.' It was an old joke but she laughed at it.

Angus did not laugh. He had turned rigid, as if struck by a poisoned dart from the blowpipe. He remembered Patel. The white-haired Tamil had applied three times and been rejected. It had been said as an excuse that he wouldn't have been suitable anyway, having no interest in sailing, boozing, gambling, and fornicating, the chief pursuits of the members. Therefore his persistent applications had been displays of anti-colonial spite. With the coming of Independence, when the Basah flag had flown above the Union Jack, he had had to be admitted. One or two had admired his courage, most had despised his snakelike pertinacity.

But why on earth had he written to Angus? They had never spoken to each other. What dreadful news had he to tell? Was Fidelia dead?

'You'd better read it,' said Janet, handing him the letter.

They watched him reading it, Nell with embarrassment and sympathy, Janet with stern suspicion. They saw how his hands shook.

He could not hide his feelings: that power had been taken from him. On his face appeared dismay, relief, pity, resentment, anger, and puzzlement. In the end the benignity of the creator was submerged in the self-pity of the victim. The demons had not been appeased after all.

'You owe her nothing,' said Nell, 'just as you owed me nothing. Like me, she took as well as gave. Like me, she knew what she was doing. If she comes here without being invited, you'd be entitled to shut the door in her face, just as you would have been entitled to shut it in mine. Isn't that so?'

Her question might have been addressed to Buddha. Certainly he paid it as much attention as the others.

'Even if she was a stranger,' said Janet, 'and came to you for help, you would give it, I hope. But she's not a stranger. She's a woman you once loved. I think you still love her. Would you have hung that painting of her in your bedroom if you didn't?'

He shook his head. What he was denying wasn't clear, even to himself.

'He was never in love with her,' said Nell, addressing Buddha. 'I say that without knowing her. But I know him. He was always too fond of himself to love anyone else. We're all too fond of ourselves, but, maybe because he's an artist, he's worse. She's married too, with a kid. Trouble, and that's what he's always avoided. No woman was worth it. Only his art mattered. Artists, he said, had to be selfish bastards. If they didn't put their work

98

first, and second, and third, they'd never produce anything worth looking at. That's what he told me, more than once.'

'He's got to help her,' said Janet.

'How can he?' asked Nell. 'This Gomez has the law on his side. As Patel says, Angus could land himself in trouble. All he wants is to get on with his painting. What's wrong with that?'

Angus managed a nod but it was a feeble one. He was devastated. Even if Fidelia and Letty did not come, his peace of mind had been destroyed. His godlike confidence in himself was gone.

'We're worrying ourselves about nothing,' said Nell, crossly. 'They won't come.'

'They will come,' said Janet, 'but they mustn't stay here. It wouldn't be safe. I'll take them to Skye with me.'

'To that cottage you told me about?' said Nell. 'That's got a marvellous view of the mountains but no electricity or running water? She'd thank you for that, I don't think.'

'To keep her child she'd live in a dungeon,' said Janet. 'Wouldn't you, Nell?'

'Well, I can tell you this, my kids wouldn't live in the dungeon with me. They like their comforts. If she swallowed her pride, she could be living in Forbes Park. Why didn't she divorce Gomez years ago? They'd have given her custody of the kid.'

'Not in the East,' said Janet. 'Women have no rights there, as Mr Patel says. Besides, she's a Catholic and doesn't believe in divorce. Neither do I. She'd be safe in Skye.'

'Until her visa expired. Where would she go then? Wherever she goes, Gomez's lawyers will find her.'

Angus then got to his feet, shakily. He put his hands to his head. He muttered that he was going out for a little while.

No, said Nell, it would be better if he stayed in and helped with the dishes. In her experience, dirty dishes were more of a help than sunsets when it came to facing up to unpleasant facts.

Later, after midnight, when they were all in bed and the house was lit by the moon, Janet waited and listened, suspiciously. Angus had remained disconsolate all evening, in spite of Nell's efforts to cheer him up. Would she make still another?

Sure enough, Nell's door could be heard opening, very quietly. Whatever her purpose, she did not want Janet to know. But loose floorboards squeaked under her heavy weight. The handle of Angus's door rattled as she turned it. The door opened with creaks like sighs.

'Sleeping, honey?' she whispered.

A groan answered.

'Would you like me to come in beside you, so that we could comfort each other? Janet's asleep, sound as Dracula's wife. She's a rum bitch, that one.'

There was a long loud contented sigh. She was in bed with Angus.

What hypocrites, thought Janet. Just a few hours ago Nell was bleating how much she was missing Bruce, and now she's in bed with another man. Angus has been given an opportunity to make himself a better man and therefore surely a better painter. And what is he doing? Putting lechery before compassion.

Janet got out of bed and like a ghost in the moonlight crept towards Angus's door, which was not quite closed.

The two within were so engrossed in what they were doing to hear her.

'This is just between you and me, honey.' said Nell. 'Nobody else will ever know.'

'Thanks, Nell. But I don't think I'm able. Too much on my mind.'

'I know. There's a lot on mine too. This is to get it off our minds, for tonight anyway. Don't worry. I'll get you going. You often were a slow starter.'

'Would it be despicable of me, Nell, if I was to tell her, if she came, that I could do nothing for her?'

'I don't want to talk about her. But it wouldn't be despicable at all. It would be sensible. Don't look at her. Look at me. Don't think about her. Think about me. Or think about your painting. I'll not be jealous. If I think about Bruce, you'll not be jealous, will you? See, you're able all right. If this isn't making love, what is? Here we are, two people, with animosity towards nobody. Isn't that love?'

Outside the room Janet's own animosity faltered, when it ought to have been growing stranger. The pair inside were committing a sin. Nell was an adulteress, Angus a fornicator. In Biblical times they would have been stoned to death. Yet they were both in a state of grace, forgetting each other's faults, forgiving all those who had ever harmed them, and wishing well to the whole world.

It was, she felt vaguely, a lesson to her.

16

Though they did not know it and never would, the inhabitants of Ardnave were the cause that night of dissension in the Free Kirk manse.

It so happened that a few days ago Mrs McPherson, she who wore hats shaped like chamberpots, had read in a woman's magazine an article on the joys of marital love-making, and had reflected that Dugald must have used her – that was the only fair way to put it – with nothing but a grunt beforehand and without asking for permission, thousands of times, and she had experienced none of the pleasure that she ought to have done. What made it worse was that he had taken it for granted that that was how the Lord had meant it to be: the man enjoying, and the woman enduring. He would share a bar of chocolate with her. Why then was he so selfish and greedy when it came to love-making?

That night in bed, with his jaws champing in a way that had irritated her for years, he announced that he was going out to Ardnave tomorrow to visit the wrath of God on the head of McAllister, that collector of idolatrous objects and the perverter of married women, for it had been observed by Mrs McCutcheon of the licensed grocer's that the big red-haired Australian woman had been wearing a wedding ring.

She waited, counted up to ten inwardly, and then retorted, in a tone of voice that he had never heard before, that he was going to do nothing of the kind. Those three persons were not members of his congregation and had nothing to do with him. If he did not mind making an officious fool of himself, she did: people were too ready to associate her with him. Nobody knew that she had opinions of her own. She had almost reached the stage when she hardly knew it herself. From now on, if he didn't mind, or rather, whether he minded or not, she was going to speak for herself even if it meant contradicting him. She then asked, after a long pause, during which his champing died away, if he would swear on the Bible that it was their wickedness he condemned and not their happiness he envied.

This attack on him by his hitherto obedient and pious wife of 35 years, just after he had said a lengthy prayer, was the most cataclysmic experience of his life. He sought explanations or excuses, for in his own way he loved her. She was 61, well past the menopause: so that could not be the reason. Did she have a secret cancer? She had a better appetite than he and walked more briskly. Could it be her childlessness? But had he not assured her time and time again that he did not blame her, that it was simply the will of God which had to be accepted without bitterness? It was not possible that she preferred some other man to him. He could think of none in Kildonan likely to be attracted to her. As she had got older she had got less comely and her temper shorter.

He was interrupted by her suddenly reminding him of the occasion two years ago when she had caught him spying through binoculars at three young women sunbathing with the tops of their costumes off. He had said that he had been looking at some Arctic terns and she had pretended to believe him. But she had not believed him. She had known that it was lust. If he had confessed, she would have loved him for it.

While he was struggling with that accusation, like a man drowning in a deep pool, she added that for her part she wished the people at Ardnave well. If he prayed to have them punished, she would pray for his prayer not to be heeded.

104

17

When Janet got up in the morning, she knew what she had to do that day. The first thing was to pack her suitcase in readiness. She would take it when she went to meet Fidelia and Letty at the airport. She intended to persuade them that it would be unwise for them to stay at Ardnave with Angus since Gomez or his lawyers would be sure to appear with warrants. It would be much safer for them to return immediately to Glasgow. She would go with them. They would stay with her in her house in Clarkston for a few days and then she would take them to Skye. Her parents would put them up until her cottage was got ready. Not even Gomez's skilful and cunning lawyers would find them there.

She told the others of these plans at breakfast. As she had expected, after last night's misconduct they were reluctant to look her, or each other, in the eye. The love they had made then was gone and had been replaced by, in Nell's case, self-disgust, and in Angus's, self-pity.

She could not resist saying, sarcastically: 'You want to get on with your painting, Angus. Don't you? Nell can make you your meals. I'll arrange with my cousin David to have the car picked up at the airport and brought back here.'

'They'll not be on the plane,' muttered Nell. 'But it's no good talking to you.'

Then Angus, to Janet's surprise and indignation, mumbled that if there was any possibility of Fidelia being on the plane he would have to go and meet it.

'What about your painting?' she sneered. 'Yesterday you couldn't spare a minute away from it.'

'I'll never paint again.'

'That's stupid,' said Nell. 'Of course you will. When we've all gone and left you in peace. All right. We'll all go to the airport. It'll be an outing, anyway. On the way back, you can show me the island.'

Janet saw her plans being ruined. 'But, Angus, if she sees you, she might want to come here. It would be better if I went alone.'

'Well, you're not going alone,' said Nell. 'We're going with you. I want to see your face when they don't come off that plane.'

Afterwards, from her window upstairs, Janet saw Angus walking on the beach where she had seen the two monks. Perhaps, she thought, hundreds of years from now, someone with second sight will have a vision of him and wonder why he was looking so woebegone. The monks in her vision had been happy.

Nell came in, dressed for going to the airport. She had on a green dress and was wearing her girdle.

'About last night,' she said. 'You know what happened. It wasn't second sight though but bloody spying. I didn't hear you but I can tell from your face. You remind me of that minister with the black hat and long jaw. Well, I'd like to tell you that it's none of your fucking business.'

'No, and I'm glad it isn't. Please don't use such language. What's the good of wearing a girdle to improve your appearance if you spoil the effect with guttersnipe language?'

'My God, you're unbelievable,' gasped Nell, collapsing on to the bed. 'If it wasn't that I know you're right I'd knock your bloody head off. I used to speak as primly as you, God help me. Until I was sixteen I went to church regularly. I won a prize for Bible knowledge. So I know what's right and what's wrong. What I did last night was wrong and yet while I was doing it I had nothing but goodwill in my heart to everybody, including you. It's more complicated than you think. You make no allowances. I'm sorry for your Douglas. Is that him?'

'Yes.'

'Handsome fellow. Knows it too. Well, why not? Reminds me a bit of Bruce when he was younger. When I sent that cable, I was in a way making a promise.'

'That was how I saw it.'

'So I've broken it. I'll have to tell him.'

'How can he blame you if he's misbehaving himself?'

'If it had been anyone but Angus. He doesn't like him, you see; in fact he detests him. He once paid £200 for one of Angus's paintings so that he could use it as a dartboard. It's really Angus I'm sorry for. You saw how keen he was about this new painting. Now he seems to have lost interest. This Fidelia, she's got a lot to answer for. Do you know what I think? I think she's not as simple and easily pushed around as she lets on. She's educated and she's managed on her own for years, which isn't easy for a woman in the East, especially if she's separated from her husband and has a kid to bring up. I've met them before that were a mixture of Catholic beliefs and heathen superstitions: a dangerous combination. So I agree with Patel. Angus should have nothing to do with her.'

'You forget that he loves her. Look at him now. Down on the beach yonder.'

Nell got up and looked out of the window. 'Poor bugger. That letter's destroyed him.'

'It needn't, if he acts honourably.'

'There you go again. Don't you know, hasn't your second sight told you, that a person can see what's the right thing to do without being able to do it? We're what we are. We might want to be different but we can't bring it about just by wanting. I wish to Christ we could.'

★   ★   ★

Angus did not object when Janet said that she would drive. He looked as if he would welcome a crash into a stone dyke or a somersault over a cliff, with an end to all self-questioning. Nell, however, who, in spite of everything, thought she had a lot to live for, expressed alarm as they shot round blind corners too fast or came off the road on to the grass verge.

It was another splendid day. The island shone and the sea glittered. The furniture of heaven could not be more magnificent.

In Kildonan they drove past the Free Kirk manse, a grim grey stone house with stunted trees in the garden. In the street people seeing the now-notorious blue Triumph 2000 stared censoriously, but one or two waved cheerfully. They might not approve of artists who painted bridges that did not look like bridges and they had been schooled since infancy to condemn sin, particularly if it took a sexual form, but they could not help feeling exhilarated by a way of life that escaped the trammels of their own. In a film or book they would enjoy the adventures of an artist who collected heathen idols and beautiful women. Well, here was one in reality, on their own native island. Therefore they waved.

At the airport was the usual group of people waiting to greet friends or board the plane.

There were some jocular remarks among them about the eccentric painter from Ardnave in his green suit and white hat, and his two girlfriends. Was he here to welcome another female to his harem? Did he have it in mind to set up a community like the Mormons, with himself the patriarch, tended hand and foot by handsome women? John McIntosh, a farmer and the owner of two working bulls, doubted whether the skinny fellow had the balls to keep one woman happy much less a dozen or so, and he said so, though in a more roundabout way, for his wife beside him was one of Mr McPherson's strictest adherents. All of the women were shocked by this suggestion of sinful polygamy but at least one of them was thinking that it might be fine having others to help with the housework and the weans, and the most tedious duties of all, those performed in bed.

The plane arrived on time. Among the passengers was no dark-faced woman in a blue coat, accompanied by a dark-faced girl in a white one.

'Well, you got it wrong,' jeered Nell.

'They'll come tomorrow,' said Janet.

'Or the day after? Or the day after that? How long before you give up, Janet?'

'They'll come tomorrow.'

Angus did not know whether he was feeling disappointment or relief, so he showed both on his face.

'Well, that's that,' said Nell, as they made their way to the car. 'Now that we've got the rest of the day to ourselves, what are we going to do with it? I'd like to take a tour of the island. That's to say, Angus, if you don't want to get back to your painting.'

'No, no. I told you I've given it up.'

'Bullshit. You'll be back at it tomorrow keener than ever. Aren't there ruined castles and holy places that we can visit? Let's pick up some food and a bottle or two of wine and Coke and have a picnic on a beach somewhere. Isn't there one that's said to be haunted?'

'If we call in at the hotel, they would give us packed lunches,' said Janet.

'Good idea. You drive, Angus.'

In the lounge bar David himself was in attendance. He was solemn when being introduced to Nell and turned more so when she asked genially if his jockstrap was tartan like his bowtie.

To Janet he whispered, when the others were out of earshot: 'Douglas phoned. He's in Birmingham, but he's still coming here on Saturday. You'll have to leave Ardnave before then.'

The drama might not be over by then. 'Maybe,' she said, and went to join the others.

109

Angus had a half-pint of lager, and Nell a glass of Coca-Cola.
'I'd like to show you my mother's grave,' he said, suddenly.
Nell could not help laughing. 'I'd love to see it, Angus. So
would Janet, I'm sure.'

Gloomily he wondered why she had laughed, indeed was still
laughing. She liked him and she wished him well, which did not
always follow. She was good-hearted and she knew that his
mother had died when he was only ten. She had seen him weep
as he remembered her. She had not laughed callously. It must
have been because she was thinking of her husband and children,
whom she loved and who were alive. Her laughter was not an
insult to him but a salute to love and life. His mother had often
laughed like that.

Before they left she went to the ladies' to take off her girdle.

18

As they set off, Angus driving, at Nell's insistence, the sadness and despair that he had felt when making the same journey 33 years ago descended upon him again. It had been January then, with snow on the ground and the sky cloudy. Though it was warm and sunny now with blue skies, he kept shivering.

Beside him Nell patted his thigh.

The driver's whiskers had had white in them. In his bewilderment Angus had wondered if it was frost. His name was Geordie McLachlan and he had kept taking fly swigs of whisky. Only Angus had noticed. Geordie had winked. Angus's father's eyes had been frozen with grief, so that they saw nothing and tears could not flow, not then or any time afterwards. The other person in the big black car, which had smelled of leather polish had been his mother's sister, Aunt Isobel from Dumfries, herself long since dead. She had kept sniffing, so regularly that Angus, counting, had found that the sniffs were exactly five seconds apart, like the flashes of the Sanaig Light.

The misery in the car had been like an enormous lump of ice.

When someone you loved and on whom you had depended died, you never completely recovered. Angus had discovered that as a small boy and he still knew it as a grown man. Perhaps it had something to do with his unwillingness or inability to let any other person become as dear to him and as indispensable. Was he making this pilgrimage to his mother's grave in an attempt to find out if Fidelia, for instance, could take his mother's place?

They came to a steep brae. Geordie had had to be cautious

here, for the surface had been slippery. Today it was dry and safe, with the hedgerows fragrant with meadowsweet, cow parsley, honeysuckle, and foxgloves. Then, they had been bare. Butterflies twinkled. Then, it had been flakes of snow.

A sandy track led from the main road to the graveyard, which was close to the sea. Among the dunes on either side rabbits darted about. It was said that, after the myxomatosis, their fur was silkier but their flesh was still suspect. It was curious how seeing them healthy and lively today comforted not only him as he was now but also as he had been all those years ago. There had been no rabbits to be seen then.

The track stopped at a wide flat green space among the dunes. Here the mourners had gathered, waiting to follow the coffin to the grave. Bottles of the island's own malts had been passed round. When empty, they had been tossed into a deep hole like a golf-course bunker. Indeed, the golf course was not far distant. Its red flags could be seen. There had been a reverent wiping of mouths.

In the graveyard, which had a wall round it protecting it from sheep, the gravelled paths were very narrow. Coffin-bearers often stumbled on to the edges of graves. None of the gravestones was grandiose. The oldest were slates, not unlike those used in the school 50 years ago. The rest were of ordinary stone, not marble or granite, and were badly worn by wind and rain. The few people on Flodday who could afford marble and fancy lettering had to do without them here where they would have been out of place.

Nell thought it all too stark, and said so. She preferred a cemetery with trees and shrubs and flowers and tombstones with winged angels.

Janet came behind them, in silence, as if, muttered Nell, she had just risen up out of a grave. A graveyard, she added, not altogether facetiously, must be a terrifying place for someone with second sight.

Angus's mother's was in a corner near the sea-wall. There the graves were 30 to 40 years old, not ancient enough to be of historic interest but not recent enough to be visited frequently.

Nell took off her shoes and walked barefoot over the grassy graves.

Janet cried, like an offended ghost: 'You are being disrespectful, Mrs Ballantyne.'

'Go to hell,' murmured Nell, and smiled, for, according to their own strict theology, a good many of the folk under her feet were already there. It was, however, too splendid a day for pessimistic eschatology, and she was feeling so hopeful about Bruce being glad to get her cable that, since she did not know any cheerful hymns, she hummed 'Waltzing Matilda'.

The last time Angus had been there, about a month ago, he had used a sharp-edged stone to scrape the moss and lichen off the inscription on his mother's headstone. They had already begun to grow again. His father had asked the stonemason to write simply: Margaret McAllister, aged 32, wife of Duncan and mother of Angus. For no extra charge he could have had a word or two of Christian consolation added but he had declined. His own name and age had been added ten years ago.

'Is your father buried here too?' said Nell. 'You didn't mention that.'

'He died in Glasgow.'

'But wanted to be buried beside your mother?'

It had been his mother's wish. Profoundly atheistic, his father had seen no virtue in the mingling of rotten bones.

'Would you mind if we gathered flowers and put them on the grave?' asked Nell. 'There are lots on the shore.'

'They don't last when pulled,' said Janet.

'They'll last long enough.'

'You'll ruin your dress.'

That, thought Nell, was a very earthly remark for a ghost. And yet many of the women buried here would have been very careful with their best clothes.

113

'Who cares?' she cried, and kilting up her dress went to the wall and clambered laboriously over it.

Leaving Angus to grieve by the grave, Janet followed Nell over the wall, but more nimbly.

She announced the names of the flowers: gowans, flag, silverweed, loosestrife, vetch, and thrift.

As she and Nell went about gathering them, with sea-birds screaming above their heads, they looked up now and then and saw Angus standing by the grave.

His mother was giving him the good advice that he had known she would. The very larks in the sky, this green-backed beetle, every living creature bound by nature's laws, were giving it too. Fidelia was not his own kind. Her background was so utterly dissimilar to his own. Her very colour was different. She was a Catholic too, with beliefs that he thought preposterous, and she had a child.

Little Letty had not liked him three years ago and probably disliked him still more now that she was older. He had not blamed her. Her jealousy had been understandable, but it had caused distasteful scenes.

Above all, Fidelia had been too ready to remind him, in that tragic voice, that Gomez was her husband in the eyes of God and would be till she or he died. She had even said it when she and Angus were making love. Too often when kissing her he had tasted tears. She had loved him, it would be caddish to deny that, but her love had had poison in it: that too had to be said. It had brought him more woe than joy. To be fair, it had inspired him to paint what up till yesterday he had regarded as his masterpiece, her portrait; but as against that it had made him lose heart and give up 'Taurus'.

Better, therefore, all things considered, to hope, here by his mother's grave, where surely he must be truthful, that Fidelia did not come, and, if she did, that he would have the honesty and strength of mind to send her away again, for all their sakes.

He had just reached this sad, bitter, but courageous decision when Nell arrived with a large bunch of wild flowers. Her face was flushed, her legs were scratched, in her hair were fragments of dry seaweed, her dress was crumpled, and her oxters were damp with sweat. There was no mystery about her. No demons threatened her. Angus was glad she had come, especially as her visit was not to be prolonged.

If she did not have uncanny intuitions, she had eyes. 'What's the matter?' she asked.

'What do you mean?'

'Have you been crying? Well, why shouldn't you have been crying if you've been remembering your mother?'

She had brought with her a swarm of flies. They pestered her as she strewed the flowers on the grave. She swore at them.

Janet was standing in the sea, scattering flowers. Like Proserpina, he thought: except that Pluto's chariot would come surging up out of the sea, drawn by sea-monsters.

'I don't think we should have our picnic here,' said Nell. 'Janet was saying there's a famous bay not far away. Red sands. Fantastically shaped rocks. Masses of white flowers. Let's go there.'

'Did she say why it was famous?'

'I thought because it was beautiful.'

'So it is, but there's another reason.'

Nearly four centuries ago marauders from an island to the north had herded into Saligo Bay more than 100 men, women, and children, and slaughtered them. It was their blood, so legend said, that had given the sand its peculiar redness, and had caused such luxuriance of gowans. Last summer Mr McPherson had held a service there, well attended though the bay could only be reached on foot. His purpose had been to exorcise the evil and console the desolate ghosts, once and for all. Unfortunately heavy rain had come on and everyone had been soaked. The bay had not been purged of its sinister associations.

115

19

The path wound among sand dunes. Blue butterflies were everywhere, as they had been on the Sunday years ago when Angus and his parents had made their pilgrimage to the bay. He explained to Nell that everyone on Flodday felt obliged to visit it at least once. Some who delayed it too long hirpled there in old age or had to be carried. It was a sacred yet ominous place. Almost everyone born on the island had ancestors among those cruelly murdered.

Though Nell sturdily did not believe in ghosts or evil spirits, she was immediately aware of them as she stood on the last dune and looked down on the little bay. Yet on that warm still afternoon it could not have looked more peaceful. The rocks, said to be like deformed animals, at that distance were simply rocks, with nothing fearsome about them. Where the sand ended, a sea of gowans began: there were many thousands of them. The immaculacy of the sand was as striking as its redness. In its shining midst was a single white object.

A dead gannet, said Angus. Sometimes when diving for fish they misjudged and broke their necks.

It wasn't a place, thought Nell, glancing aside at Janet, for anyone who claimed to have second sight. If you didn't actually see ghosts, you'd have to pretend that you did and the result would be the same.

There were despairing cries, as of people being killed. They were made by sea-birds.

'It's beautiful,' said Nell, 'but I wouldn't like to come here alone. Why did they kill them?'

'Revenge,' said Angus. 'About thirty years before that, Flodday men had made a similar bloody raid on their island.'

'After thirty years?'

'The desire for revenge is deep-rooted.'

'Not with me it isn't. I never bear grudges.'

They found a comfortable hollow and spread out the rug and picnic things. Janet did not offer to help. She wandered off, as if in a trance, towards the rocks. One of them, Nell thought, was like a gigantic frog.

'We'll start without her,' said Nell. 'I'm famished.'

They ate the dainty hotel sandwiches. Angus drank wine and Nell Coca-Cola. Bruce, she said, wouldn't believe his eyes if he saw her. She used to be a terrible boozer. But it was having an effect, her abstinence. She might not look it but she had lost half a stone since leaving Sydney two months ago.

'About last night, Angus,' she said.

'I thought we weren't going to talk about last night.'

'I didn't use anything. Nor did you.'

He didn't feel worried, so he didn't look it. He smiled.

'I'm not past having a kid, you know. I still have my periods. I'm only forty-four. Lots of women have kids at that age.'

He stopped smiling. 'If you knew that, why didn't you take precautions?'

'I didn't want to. I didn't feel like it. What a laugh if I was pregnant by you, Angus.'

'A laugh!'

'It'd knock your selfish attitude all to hell. I'd be home in time for Bruce to think it was his. I think I could arrange that. But what if it had frightened blue eyes and a wee huffy mouth? He'd know it was yours then.'

'This conversation is in bad taste, Nell.'

'I wonder what he'd do if he found out that the kid was yours. You're not his favourite person, as you know.'

'I refuse to consider such a possibility.'

'He wouldn't disown it. He's fond of kids. He wouldn't blame it. In fact, it might bring him and me closer. He'd think I was in trouble, real trouble, and he would want to stand by me.'

'Let's talk about something else, please. Or rather let us not talk at all but enjoy the peace and quiet.'

'Wouldn't you be proud if in a year or two I was to send you photographs of your son or daughter? Which would you like it to be?'

Such a foolish question deserved to be ignored.

'But if you didn't do the trick last night, you never will, not with me anyway. From now on I'm a chaste married woman. But there's Janet. She's a beautiful woman, as you've no doubt noticed. But I guess you'd have to have wings and a prick of gold. Where is she, anyway?' She stood up to look. 'She seems to have vanished.'

'There's a cave. She'll have gone into it.'

'Yes, that's what she must have done. What's she hiding from, do you think?'

'It's hardly a place to hide in. It's said to be haunted, like the bay. Some of the victims tried to escape into it. Bones have been dug up. Human bones.'

'Jesus, certainly not a place to hide in. Not if you're normal, that is. You know, there are times when I feel that it wouldn't take much to send her completely round the bend.'

'She had an aunt who went insane.'

'Maybe it's in the family, like second sight. We'll have to go and look for her.'

'In a little while. We'll have a rest first.'

'I expect she's safe enough.'

They lay down and sunbathed for half an hour.

Nell got to her feet, feeling anxious. There was still no sign of Janet.

She kicked Angus's foot. 'Better get up. She's not to be seen. Does that cave go far in?'

'Yes, but nobody knows how far. Apparently the passage is very low and narrow. Bones were found in it too.'

'Some poor bugger went in and died there?'

'Probably.' He got up and knocked the sand off his slacks and shirt. 'I don't like caves, any caves. I get claustrophobic.'

They set off across the sands. When they came to the dead gannet, Nell touched it with her bare toes.

Live gannets were diving into the sea. They watched one come up with a fish.

'Her Douglas is coming on Saturday,' said Nell, as they moved on. 'I'll be interested to meet him. She says he's a karate expert.'

'I have no wish to meet the egregious Douglas.'

Nell laughed. 'I should think not, considering that he might want to break your neck. I know that you haven't ravished Janet but, Douglas, I think, has got such a high opinion of himself that, though he'd have to break your neck if you'd ravished his wife, he'd regard it as an insult to him if you hadn't, and so he'd have to break your neck in any case.'

Nell spoke nervously. They were now among the strangely shaped rocks. The one like a huge frog had lumps of quartzite for eyes. She kept imagining people with their throats cut and their blood seeping into the sand.

As they approached the cave they began to shout Janet's name. At least the tide was well out.

They stood at the mouth and looked in. It was as big as a small church. The ceiling was high. On the wall was written in large white letters: JESUS SAVES. 'Well, he didn't, did he?' muttered Nell. They saw bones in a corner. A cow's, whispered Angus. Cattle often came down on to the sand in hot weather.

There were fresh footprints, Janet's, no doubt, going towards

120

the back of the cave, where the roof sloped down. In the green slimy wall at floor level was a small opening. A sheep would have had difficulty in squeezing through. Yet Janet must have done it.

'Do you think you could try, Angus?' asked Nell. 'I'm too fat.'

He almost protested that he would make a mess of his white shirt and tan slacks. It would have been a sensible, if craven, complaint.

He turned and looked out at the beauty of light and the vastness of space.

Then, crouching like a foetus, and whimpering, he crept through the hole into a passage where the roof could not have been more than three feet high and the sides were even less than that apart. The floor was rough with stones. He shouted Janet's name, but the noise confused and frightened him.

It wasn't likely that the roof which had stood for thousands, perhaps millions, of years would collapse in the next two or three minutes, but he couldn't be certain. If, as many believed, there was an end to time and God one day blew His trumpet summoning all corpses, from those of mountaineers buried in the snows of Everest to those of sailors in wrecks at the bottom of the sea, his would not be able to respond. It would be like a beetle squashed under a heavy boot. His loneliness now, though terrifying, was nothing to the loneliness he imagined then, when, bidden to join the celestial throng, he was not able. It did not help, on the contrary, it increased his terror, that he did not believe in God or resurrection.

After about 20 yards, he could go no further. He heard a scream. It came from his own mouth but it was the demons screaming. They were mocking him. Look at him, they were saying, he's no better than a worm and yet he had the arrogance to think himself capable of creating immortal masterpieces. His legs being too weak to support him, he had to get down on to his stomach, like a worm indeed. He began wriggling backwards, desperately. He might not have had the strength for the last yard or two if Nell hadn't seized his shoes and pulled him out.

121

He lay gasping, on his stomach, not willing to let Nell see his face still contorted by terror.

She took hold of him and heaved him up on to his feet. She couldn't help laughing when she saw his face. 'My God, Angus, your nose is bleeding.'

And his legs were aching, his head throbbed where it had bumped against the roof, his left elbow was bruised, and his clothes were ruined.

She helped him to the mouth of the cave, where his legs gave way. He sat with his back against the wall, looking out at the bright sky.

'Poor Angus,' she said. 'No wonder you're wary of women. I wonder where that crazy bitch has got to. You couldn't see anything?'

'Nothing.' He really meant nothing: sheer black nihility. Dimly, in the depths of his disordered mind, there appeared an idea for a painting.

They were so intent, Angus on recovering from the horror, and Nell on wiping the blood from his face, that neither of them noticed Janet emerge from the hole, on hands and knees. She got to her feet, a little unsteadily, stretched herself like a cat, and came towards them.

Nell turned her head, saw her, and yelled. The very fact that Janet was suddenly there, as if she had materialised out of air, was shocking enough. What made it more so was that her face and hair were green. Most frightening of all, she was smiling at them, not at all like a zombie who had just been visiting other zombies, but cheerfully, like a holiday-maker a little more venturesome than her companions.

'It's a pity I didn't bring a torch,' she said. 'There's an inner chamber, from the feel of it larger than this.'

'You've got a bloody cheek,' said Nell, 'frightening us like that. Poor Angus tried to go in after you. He's not recovered yet.'

'Douglas and I once explored a cave in Skye. We went in for

half a mile. We had torches, of course. Douglas is afraid of nothing.'

Which meant, thought Nell, that he had no imagination. Just as well, married to this witch.

20

Angus and Nell decided, in a consultation while Janet was out of the room, to make no fuss about her going to the airport. Better humour her until Saturday when Douglas, rash fellow, was coming to claim her. They would not accompany her. There would be no satisfaction this time in seeing her face when Fidelia and Letty were not among the passengers. Perhaps they ought to be there in case the disappointment was too much for her, but they hadn't yet recovered from the ordeal in the cave. They needed a rest from her.

They noticed that she did not put her suitcase into the car. Nell could not resist mentioning it.

'So you've dropped the idea of going with them to Glasgow?'

'I can't stop them coming here. I should have known that.'

They went out to watch her drive off.

'Well, Angus, what are you going to do now? Me, don't laugh, I'm going to do a little jogging. I've got to get some more flab off. Why don't you do some painting?'

He shook his head listlessly, but when she came downstairs wearing brief shorts, sweatshirt, and sandshoes he was in his studio. Careful not to disturb him, she set off across the machair at a gentle trot. Only sheep and larks saw her, thank God. Soon she was drenched with sweat, for the day was warm. Flies were quickly attracted to such a feast. They buzzed about her eyes and ears. One even entered her mouth. For Bruce's sake, she persevered.

After half an hour she took a short rest and then turned back,

looking forward to a dip in the sea as her reward. How, she
wondered, as she puffed and panted, did flies manage to keep up
with her and yet keep circling round her head? When you came
to think of it, the most unlikely creatures had remarkable powers.
So perhaps it wasn't so incredible that certain people, such as
Janet, were able to foresee the future or have visions of the past.
And then there was Angus, so careful to supply his shrine with
breadcrumbs every night. She had laughed at his talk of demons
having to be placated, but in her own life there had been
misfortunes which weren't her own fault. She had called them
bad luck but that explained nothing. If any place was ever
haunted, it was this island. Its very beauty was uncanny. How
could it be so beautiful, considering the dreadful things that had
happened on it? Angus had told her that hundreds of years ago
monks had lived where his house was. They were said to haunt
it. He hadn't ever seen any himself but he had felt their presence.
God help her, looking out of her window last night she had seen
one herself, having a piddle. It was like her, coarse cow that she
was, to see him doing that. Other people would have seen him
praying. But of course it was nonsense, she hadn't seen him at all,
it had been imagination and moonlight.

When she arrived back at the house, soaked with sweat, Angus
was still in his studio. Pleased about that, she went quietly upstairs
for a towel, and then made for the beach, past what Angus had
said had been the monks' privy. A little blue flower grew there
which wasn't to be found in any other place on the island. She
paused to look for it among the other flowers. There it was, not
unlike a violet but with a longer stem.

If the ghosts of the holy celibates were there, watching, they
were going to get a treat. On the sand, out in the open, she
peeled off her damp shorts and sweatshirt and kicked off her
shoes. Then, naked, she ran into the sea. Since the sand shelved
gently, she had a long way to go before she could plunge in.
Therefore those invisible watchers were getting a good look at

her fat white bum as it flashed in the sun. Today fatness in females was not admired by males, hence her desire to get rid of some for Bruce's sake; but, according to Angus, in the past it had been different, a woman without a fat bum, big boobs, and plump thighs would have been considered uncomely. He had shown her paintings by famous artists like Rubens, in which the women, mostly goddesses, were rolling in fat. By those standards Nell herself would have been in demand as a model. When the water was up to her waist she turned and let them see her breasts, a bit flabby – a point of beauty, though, in medieval eyes – and big enough, as Bruce had once said, fondly, to gag a horse.

Well, she thought, as she began to swim in the chilly water, there should be more pep in their prayers tonight.

21

Meanwhile, on her way to the airport, Janet had called in at the hotel. She wanted to know more about Douglas's arrangements.

Unfortunately, it was Mary she saw, with her usual vinegary face.

'Is this you come back then?'

'No, it isn't.'

'Well, it should be. Everybody's talking about you. Even Agnes and Jean.'

Janet had to smile. Agnes was ten, Jean eight. They had a more sensible attitude to most things than their prudish and bigoted mother.

'And what are Agnes and Jean saying about me?'

'It's not funny, Janet. They keep asking what you're doing at Ardnave in that dreadful man McAllister's house.'

'Did they call him dreadful? I thought they found him amusing. And what have you been telling them, Mary?'

'What can I tell them? *I* don't know what you're doing.'

'Next time they ask just tell them I cook his meals. They're practical. They'll see the sense of that. And it happens to be true. I don't sleep with him. Yes, I know I went there with some such intention, to pay Douglas back, but I changed my mind. Anyway, I've got a chaperone now.'

'Is that what you call her? We know about her. A big red-haired Australian. She's married too. Bold and brazen, they say.'

'She knew Angus years ago in Basah. Can't people visit friends without the Kildonan gossips being bad-minded about it?'

'Why isn't her husband with her?'

'He couldn't get away.'

'How long is she staying?'

'She's returning home next week. She's eager to get back to her husband.'

'Is that why she's living with another man?'

'It could be, Mary. Love's a funny thing. That's something I've learned in the past few days. But I came in to ask about Douglas. I suppose he's staying here?'

'He's booked a double room for Saturday and Sunday. He's flying back on Monday. He expects you to be going with him.'

'Does he, now? We'll have to see about that.'

'David and I don't want any more nonsense from you, Janet. We're going to have to lie to protect you.'

'Lie if you like. I intend to tell him the truth.'

'Hasn't it occurred to you that Douglas might go out to Ardnave and assault Mr McAllister?'

'Yes, it has occurred to me. It has also occurred to Mr McAllister. He's not too happy about it. Well, I'll have to be going. I've to be at the airport to meet the plane.'

'Why? Who are you expecting?'

'Another friend of Angus's.'

'What sort of friend? A man or woman?'

'A woman. From the Philippines. With her little girl.'

Mary's mouth fell open in horror. 'Are they black?'

'Would it make any difference if they were?' she asked, scornfully.

'The girl, is McAllister her father?'

'No, he isn't. I might want to take Agnes and Jean out to Ardnave to meet her. I'm sure they'd love to come.'

'You will do nothing of the kind, Janet Maxwell.'

'I thought you were bringing them up to be Christians, Mary.'

'So I am. That is why I won't allow them to visit a house where a man is living with *three* married women.'

130

'I'm sorry, Mary, but I'll have to hurry.'

Hurry she did and was in good time for the plane. Among those who came off it were a tall dark-faced woman wearing a white skirt and blue coat and a small girl in a white coat and with a white ribbon in her hair.

If Nell had been there, dumbfounded, Janet would not have looked at her in triumph. She had nothing to do with their coming. She had just foreseen it.

That was all she had foreseen. She did not know what was going to happen now.

PART TWO

1

As he checked in at Glasgow Airport on Saturday morning, Douglas Maxwell showed no sign of impatience or anxiety. This was not because as a four-handicap golfer he had learned to control such destructive emotions, but simply because he did not feel them. Mary McNaught, when she had telephoned, had urged him to come as soon as possible, hinting at imminent disaster. He supposed she had meant that Janet was sick with worry at having deserted him, which was how it should be, but his reading of the situation was that, the longer Janet worried, the less likely she was to run away again. She was being taught a lesson. When he went to bring her back, she would be sufficiently humble.

In the airport all those, and there were many, who glanced twice at him, sometimes thrice, were struck not by any dark foreboding on his face but by bright self-confidence. In the whole of Scotland that morning there was no more handsome, healthy, or optimistic young man. He wore a smart navy-blue blazer with the red-and-gold crest of the Thornwood Golf Club, a white silk shirt, a Glasgow University tie, light blue Daks, and shoes that had cost £95. Yesterday he had had his hair trimmed and styled, his moustache clipped, and his hands manicured, in a select establishment where the assistants were thinly clad young women who had vied with one another to attend to him. It was therefore no surprise or embarrassment to him when, as he handed over his golf bag to the stewardess behind the counter, she smiled at him with undiluted admiration. He was used to such homage, but since it was deserved he did not let it go to his head.

His gracious air was more admirable than the stewardess knew. As well as his clubs he was taking a little guilty secret with him to Flodday. Most men would have been shifty-looking because of it. Douglas had never looked shifty in his life, not even when Janet had caught him practising putting with Cissie McDade.

Late last night Elsie Hamilton had telephoned to say, in her husky sexy voice, that her husband Bob had gone to London on business and she was feeling lonely. What about coming over for a drink? The kids were in bed, sound asleep.

She was an attractive woman as well as a golfer, and he had had her before, on a golf outing to St Andrews. She was a good sport who knew just how much a friendly fuck was worth. There was no undue palaver before or whiny repentance after. Also, unlike other women he knew, she had her children well trained, so that they could be depended on not to interrupt inconveniently. There was a snag. He had overcome it before but perhaps he shouldn't a second time. He knew Bob Hamilton, in fact had played golf with him, not often, for Bob's handicap was 17, but once was enough to establish some kind of kinship. As he swithered, with the telephone at his ear, Elsie had asked did he know that Bob in his cups had confessed that he had had it off with Cissie McDade recently? Douglas had not known and was indignant now that he knew. It was because of Cissie McDade that he and Janet had fallen out. Surely he was justified therefore in accepting Elsie's offer.

He had gone in his white Rover and parked it prudently two avenues away, under a big lime tree. He had not been in the Hamiltons' villa three minutes before he had a glass of Glenmorangie in his hand and Elsie, clad only in a white dressing-gown, was fiddling with his zip. A woman so keen had to be obliged without delay. So he had gone to it with zest, on top of cushions taken from the big black-and-white settee.

While he was busy, he had done some thinking. Elsie, sensible woman, had wanted only what he was giving her, just as he had wanted what she was letting him have. She had kept her mouth shut. There had been no babbling about magical forces. He had reflected, with satisfaction, that his Janet, though vexatious with her nonsense about holy communion, was too virtuous and old-fashioned to let any man, except him, do what he was now doing to Elsie.

All that thinking had not hindered his performance. Elsie had been appreciative. He had stayed for another two hours and, at her instigation, had had another go before he left. He had not quite succeeded this time but, as Elsie had said, a partial failure on his part was better than most men's successes. She had been referring to his powerful thigh muscles.

He did not intend to mention this little adventure with Elsie to Janet. His experience as a golfer had taught him to concentrate on one thing at a time.

Among the other passengers for Flodday, he noticed only one checking in golf clubs. This was a big sandy-haired paunchy man in a blue light-weight suit that looked as if it had been slept in. He spoke with an Australian accent and kept yawning. His clubs, Douglas noted, were American-made Pings, the best money could buy. Evidently he had brought them all the way from Australia. He must be keen. Yet at his age – about 50, Douglas thought – and with his belly he could hardly be very proficient. I could give him eight strokes and beat him, thought Douglas.

There were two other interesting passengers, dark-skinned foreigners, speaking a language Douglas could not identify. One was about 40, handsome in a dago fashion, with swarthy face and black moustache. Knowledgeable in such matters, Douglas saw that this man's fawn linen suit was of the best quality and cut. His shoes were Italian, even more expensive than Douglas's own. Round his hairy wrist was a gold Rolex watch. Was he going to Flodday to buy an estate there? No narrow-minded nationalist or moralist, Douglas did not mind foreigners buying up large parts of Scotland. Their wealth, if it was considerable enough, gave them that privilege. If this chap with the sweet-smelling hair, after he had bought the estate, wanted to bring over a harem of wives, good luck to him, provided he was discreet and kept them in – what was it called? – purdah, an institution that Douglas thought had a lot to commend it.

The other dago was older and more soberly dressed.

Douglas approved of people with money, for he hoped to have a lot himself one day. Towards that end, marrying Janet had been a mistake. She had brought little into the kitty and her property in Skye needed costly renovations, Moreover, she was too fond of giving his money away to charities that did not deserve it. Few charities did. On the plus side she was beautiful and her beauty was all his. Their children, when he decided it was time to have one or two, would be superior specimens. Janet, he suspected, a little uneasily, had talents still to be revealed. He had once introduced her to golf. After only half-a-dozen lessons she was able to hit the ball only thirty yards or so less than he. He had been relieved when she had suddenly lost interest in the game, calling it childish. Apart from the danger of her becoming better at it than he, which would have necessitated his giving it up, he knew the temptations that could beset golfing women. Weren't Cissie and Elsie examples?

Those were his thoughts as he boarded the plane.

He took the seat next to the Australian.

His first friendly remark was ignored but he persevered. The Scots were famous the world over for their friendliness to strangers and he must not let the side down. Besides, the Australian looked tired and depressed, and was far from home.

'This your first visit to Flodday?' asked Douglas.

'Yep.'

'It's a beautiful island. We should get a good view of it today.

Sometimes you can't see it for mist. My name's Maxwell, by the way, Douglas Maxwell.'

'Ballantyne.'

'I saw you checking in your golf clubs. You'll like the course on Flodday.'

Ballantyne showed interest. 'D'you know it?'

'I've played it several times. A links course, like St Andrews and Troon. It could be every bit as good as those if it was looked after better. Cowpats on the fairways. Sheep's droppings on the greens. That sort of thing. Not enough money spent on it. Of course, it hasn't many members. You a member of a club?'

'Wallaby Creek, Sydney.'

Douglas had never heard of it but then Ballantyne had probably never heard of Thornwood. 'Do you play often?'

'Not as often as I would like.'

'I noticed you've got Pings. Mine are Rams. May I ask what's your handicap? Mine's four. I'm still hoping to get down to scratch.'

Ballantyne was sneering. 'In Australian terms your four would be six. Our system of handicapping is the fairest in the world. Did you know that?'

Not only had Douglas not known it, he did not believe it. 'What's your then?'

'Five. A genuine five. It would be two here. I have a fight keeping to it. I guess I'm getting older and I haven't been playing so much lately.'

'Pressure of work?'

'That and other things.'

Douglas was not far behind his wife in nosiness. 'What line of business are you in, Mr Ballantyne?'

'Timber.'

Douglas laughed. 'You'll not find much of that on Flodday. There's hardly a tree. I'm in civil engineering myself. What brings you to Flodday?'

139

Ballantyne's face told him not to be so bloody inquisitive. Ballantyne's voice said, meekly enough: 'My wife's there.'

'What a coincidence! So's mine.'

'She's staying with friends at a place called Ardnave. Do you know it?'

'I've been there. It's pretty remote. Not many houses.'

'People we met in Basah years ago,' muttered Ballantyne.

'Basah? Where's that?'

'You'd say in the Far East. Not far from Indonesia. It's an island too. Do you know Flodday well?'

'My wife's relations own a hotel there.'

'That's handy. I'll need a place to stay.'

'Won't you be joining your wife at Ardnave?'

'Not right away. They were more her friends than mine. You know how it is. Name's McAllister. Do you know him? He calls himself a painter.'

'You mean an artist? Like Van Gogh?'

'What he paints is crap.'

'To tell you the truth, I think painting's a bit of a racket. If they know a painting's by somebody with a big name, like Rembrandt, they say it's worth millions. But if they don't know they say it's worth hundreds. The same painting, mind you.'

'Do you think you could get me fixed up with a room?'

'Sure. David, my wife's cousin, is meeting me at the airport. I'll introduce you to him. Maybe we could fix up a game. To find out if a Scottish four is as good as an Australian five.'

'It'll depend on Nell. That's my wife.'

'I hope she doesn't object to your playing golf? Lots of wives do. Mine does, a bit. For a ridiculous reason. She's got a crazy notion that if you play golf you can't have much of an imagination.'

'Nell doesn't mind.'

'Good. Let's fix up a game then. How long are you here for?'

'I don't know yet.'

140

'I have to return on Monday. What about this afternoon?'

'It depends on what Nell wants.'

'But you said she doesn't mind. You brought your clubs, didn't you? Provisionally, then, this afternoon, at three. Look, that's Flodday now. There's the course. D'you see the flags? Did you ever see greener turf?'

Ballantyne stared down gloomily. 'It looks pretty bare.'

'Spoken like a timber merchant.' Douglas laughed.

'Nowhere to hide.'

'Except for some caves.'

'A good place to tell the truth.'

And not a bad place either to tell judicious lies.

'I've heard there are ancient ruined churches.'

'There's one out at Ardnave. Are you a religious man?'

Ballantyne shook his head. 'When she was at school, Nell won a prize for Bible knowledge.'

Another strange remark, thought Douglas. He almost said that his Janet had second sight, but that wasn't a thing to speak about, far less boast about.

2

It was one of Douglas's jokes, frequently repeated, that it was appropriate that David McNaught should keep a stuffed penguin in his office, for with his habit of wearing black waistcoats and white collars, and with his big nose and flat feet, he looked like one. But Douglas had never seen a furtive penguin, and at the airport David was very furtive when asked why Janet hadn't come with him. Also he kept staring away from Douglas to the two dagos who were being obsequiously looked after by a chauffeur in a grey uniform with the name Ascog Castle Hotel on the front of his cap. It was one of the most exclusive and luxurious hotels in Scotland.

'Do you know who they are?' asked Douglas.

'Yes. I was talking to Mr McCrae the chauffeur. The younger one's Mr Gomez, a millionaire from Manila in the Philippines. The older one's his lawyer.'

'I thought so. Are they here to buy up some estate?'

'I understand it's a private visit.'

'Well, what about Janet? Why isn't she here to meet me? Don't tell me she's still in a huff. Or is she too ashamed of herself?'

'As a matter of fact, Douglas, she's not staying at the hotel.'

'Then where is she staying?'

'At Ardnave.'

'Ardnave?' Douglas looked about him. He couldn't see Ballantyne. 'Who's she staying with at Ardnave?'

David looked more furtive than ever. 'A family called McAuslan.' There had once been a minister in Skye called that.

'How did she come to meet them?'

'In church.'

'Oh. But she should still have come to meet me. She'll have no grumble then if I have a game of golf this afternoon with this gentleman.'

Ballantyne was coming over.

'David, this is Mr Ballantyne, from Australia. He's come to join his wife who's also staying at Ardnave, with people called McAllister. But he wants a room in the hotel for tonight.'

David's face could hold no more furtiveness. It kept spilling out. 'Mr Ballantyne,' he asked in a small voice, 'is Mrs Ballantyne expecting you?'

'I wouldn't think so. I didn't let her know.'

'I have met her. She came into the hotel, with Douglas's wife Janet.'

'So they know each other?' cried Douglas. 'That's good. They won't object then to our having a game of golf.'

'I don't think that follows,' said David, in another small voice.

'Do you know McAllister?' asked Ballantyne.

'He comes into the hotel occasionally.'

The luggage then arrived. They carried the suitcases to the car.

Douglas sat in front with David. They set off towards Kildonan.

'This McAllister,' said Ballantyne,' I don't suppose he's married.'

'No, he isn't.'

Douglas wasn't the quickest of thinkers, except when his own interests were involved. He couldn't understand how Mrs Ballantyne could be staying with the McAllister family if that family consisted only of McAllister.

'He never struck me as the marrying kind,' said Ballantyne, 'but I bet he's got some woman living with him. He likes having a woman in bed so long as he can get rid of her whenever he wants.'

Douglas knew many men like that. He was one himself. This McAllister was a man to be envied. He had the use of women

144

without any responsibility. He could throw them out as soon as they were of no more use.

'Can I hire a car in town?' asked Ballantyne. 'In case I want to drive out to Ardnave?'

'Good idea,' said Douglas. 'I'll go with you, if you don't mind. My wife's at Ardnave too, staying with a family called McAuslan. I wonder if the McAuslans know McAllister. They're bound to, the place being so isolated.'

'McDougall's garage has a car for hire,' said David.

'Maybe I should phone first.'

'Mr McAllister doesn't have a telephone.'

'Well, I could phone the McAuslans,' said Douglas.

'They haven't got a telephone either.'

'It must really be the outback,' said Ballantyne.

They stopped then at the hotel door.

Leaving David to deal with Ballantyne, Douglas, as a relative, went through to the kitchen looking for Mary. He found her supervising the preparation of lunch.

She took him to the private sitting room.

'I suppose David told you Janet's not staying at the hotel?'

'Yes. He said she's staying with people called McAuslan out at Ardnave.'

'Did he tell you that?'

'Yes. Do you know them? You must, for David said Janet met them in church.'

'Is that what he said? Now, Douglas, if you'll excuse me, I'll have to get back to the kitchen.'

'Where are Agnes and Jean?' He had always found his nieces more ready informants than their mother.

'Out playing somewhere.'

'Just a minute, Mary. On the telephone you seemed to be hinting that, if I didn't come immediately, there could be trouble. What did you mean? What kind of trouble?'

145

'You did not come immediately. This is Saturday. I telephoned on Wednesday.'

'I couldn't just drop everything.'

'Neither can I. Speak to David. She's *his* cousin.'

She went out but came back briefly to tell him that he had been put into No. 18.

He felt annoyed, not so much at Mary, for she had a hotel to run, but at Janet, who was putting him to all this inconvenience under the silly impression that she was getting her own back. Also, if he remembered rightly, Room 18 was one of the few that did not have a view of hills and sea. It was true that as a relative he would not be paying for it, but that was no excuse. It was again Janet's fault. In some way she had offended Mary and he was being made to suffer for it.

3

Meanwhile, David had conducted Ballantyne to his room on the top floor. It had a double bed which Ballantyne, with a curious shyness, had requested. He did not look a shy man. There was a fine view of the harbour and across the sea-loch. Ballantyne stood looking out, wistfully. He was not a wistful man either.

'Can you see Ardnave from here?' he asked.

'I'm afraid not. It's too far west.'

'You said you met my wife, Mr McNaught.'

'Just the once, briefly.'

'I shouldn't ask you, for how should you know, but do you think she'll be pleased to see me?'

'I'm sure she will. I believe she sent you a cable.'

'When?'

'Two days ago. You must have left before it arrived.'

'Why was she sending me a cable? She's not in trouble, is she?'

'No. I think it was to say that she was returning home next week. So Janet told me.'

'Is she friendly with Janet?'

'Yes.'

'That's good. She was supposed to be away for four months.'

'She must be feeling homesick.'

'Do you think so? This other woman that McAllister's got living with him, do you know her?

David decided that it would be better to let Ballantyne, and Douglas too, find out for themselves what was going on. He had compromised himself enough already.

'Yes, I know her. I'm going out to Ardnave myself this afternoon. I could give Mrs Ballantyne a message if you like.'

'Thanks. Just tell her I'd be very pleased if she would join me for dinner tonight.'

'I'll tell her. I'm sure she'll be delighted.'

'Will you be seeing McAllister – no, never mind, I'll have to deal with him myself. Well, I'm much obliged to you, Mr McNaught. I wonder if you'd ask young Maxwell if he'd like to have lunch with me. He talked about a game of golf this afternoon but maybe he'll be in too big a hurry to meet his wife.'

'I think he'll be able to play. He's not meeting Janet till this evening.'

'Maybe we can all have dinner together.'

With flat-footed speed David went downstairs and locked himself in his office. He needed to be alone for a few minutes to consider how he could get away with his lies about the McAuslans. He would need Janet's co-operation. She might give it too enthusiastically and talk at length about her hosts, the mythical McAuslans, but on the other hand she might prefer to tell Douglas the truth.

David did not know if Janet had been to bed with McAllister, but he thought it unlikely, or if Mrs Ballantyne had, which he thought very likely. Mrs Ballantyne had looked the kind of woman who would willingly comfort a man in that way, whereas Janet, of course, was not that kind of woman at all. With most to forgive, Ballantyne would do it gladly, being eager to be reconciled with his wife, but Douglas, though in the wrong, would be incensed and might rush out to Ardnave looking for revenge. McAllister was innocent in that the two women, or rather the three women, had descended upon him uninvited, but that might not save him from having his nose punched by Ballantyne or his bones broken by Douglas. Having forgiven his wife, Ballantyne might still want to punish her seducer, even if he suspected she had done the seducing, while

Douglas was always looking for an opportunity to use his karate skills in earnest.

Then there was the advent of Gomez and his lawyer. Janet had explained Mrs Gomez's position. David had got a glimpse of her and her daughter in the car at the door of the hotel on Thursday, on their way out to Ardnave. He had been touched by her sadness.

4

Ballantyne and Douglas had lunch together at a table in a corner of the dining-room. Saying that he might soon have something to celebrate, Ballantyne ordered a bottle of the hotel's best wine, but before he had drunk so much as a glassful, he was talkative, more like the brash coarse-tongued Australian Douglas would have expected.

The golf match was arranged for three o'clock. Douglas had telephoned the secretary of the club at his home to book the tee for that hour but had been told it wasn't necessary. He was reminded that the green fees were to be put into the box in the shed.

'How about thirty pounds to the winner, and a fiver for every birdie?' said Ballantyne.

Such large sums were ungentlemanly. 'Isn't that rather a lot?' said Douglas.

'Come off it, Maxwell. You think you can knock hell out of an old man like me.'

Douglas wished he would speak less loudly and use politer language. Two silvery-haired old ladies at a nearby table were well within hearing. So were other guests, without much straining of their ears.

'As amateurs we play for fun, don't we?' he said.

'I play to win. Always. But if the idea of money changing hands offends you, how about this? I'm having dinner tonight with Nell. Why don't you and Janet join us? The loser pays the bill. Excluding booze.'

Douglas could not bear to say that his wife, thrawn besom, might refuse to come. Nor could he point out that the bill could amount to more than £50. For the sake of his country he must not appear hen-pecked or mean. So he nodded.

'Good. I want to meet your Janet, to thank her for being friendly with Nell.'

By this time Ballantyne was on his third glass of wine. Douglas was still sipping his first: he did not approve of drinking before a game. If Ballantyne was beaten, he would claim it was because he was drunk.

'I'm going to tell you something, Maxwell, that I ought to keep to myself. I don't know if Nell will show up tonight. She didn't come to UK just to visit her sister. It was also to get away from me.'

Douglas managed to look shocked and sympathetic. 'I'm sorry to hear that, old man.'

'She'd got it into her head I didn't want her any more. I guess I was doing a bit of fucking around. She was drinking too much and letting herself go to fat.'

The two old ladies were fairly enjoying their roast lamb.

'Her age, the doctor said. Menopausal stress. Poor Nell. Have you any kids, Maxwell?'

'Not yet.'

'Are you waiting till your handicap's in double figures?'

Douglas laughed. 'I'll be sixty before that happens. If you've got a good solid swing, it never leaves you.'

But Douglas was not thinking about golf. Himself invulnerable because of Janet's peculiar attitude to sex, he was wondering, with a malicious little thrill, about Mrs Ballantyne's relationship with McAllister. Had she come, fat though she was, to find revenge in McAllister's bed?

Douglas's own roast lamb was delicious.

'Nell met this turd McAllister in Basah. Let me tell you, Maxwell, when she was young Nell was magnificent. Marvellous

152

body. Masses of red hair. Gutsy sense of humour. Lion-hearted. If it had been any other cunt than McAllister she'd gone to, I don't think I would have minded so much, but he's a selfish bastard. He takes all right but he doesn't want to give. Artists say they've got to be selfish bastards if they're going to turn out masterpieces but his paintings are a lot of crap, so he's a selfish bastard under false pretences, if you see what I mean.'

Someone in the dining-room tut-tutted loudly.

'For heaven's sake, old man,' whispered Douglas, 'take it easy. Ladies present.'

'I don't mind telling you I came here intending to wring his neck but I don't feel like that now. In fact, if he's helped Nell in any way, I might even thank him. Let somebody else give him his comeuppance.'

Douglas heard someone mutter that he was going to complain to the management. One of the old ladies, though, gave him a wink.

Ballantyne ordered another bottle. 'Tell me about your wife, Maxwell. What's she doing on Flodday without you?'

Douglas was instantly defensive, not on Janet's behalf but his own. 'She wanted a little break, that's all.'

'Funny her not staying at the hotel her cousin owns.'

'Janet likes quiet places. It's very quiet out at Ardnave.'

'I've got the impression she's got a mind of her own.'

Douuglas smiled warily but said nothing.

'Like all the Scotch, Maxwell, you're too buttoned up. I would say, looking at you, that appearances mean a hell of a lot to you. Am I right?'

Whether or not it was meant as a compliment, Douglas took it as one.

'As long as the neighbours don't know. That's the principle you Scotch go by.'

'With a name like Ballantyne, your ancestors must have been Scottish.'

153

'My grandfather came from Ayrshire, my grandmother from Carnoustie. There's a good golf course there.'

'There are lots of good courses in Ayrshire.'

'To get back to your wife, Maxwell, is she just having a little break or has she run away from you?'

'Don't be ridiculous. What gave you that idea?'

'You did. You spend a lot of money on that face, but it's easy to read. Is loyalty important to you, Maxwell?'

'Loyalty to my country, do you mean?'

'Hell, no. That's easy. I meant loyalty to your wife. I'm sorry to say I've let Nell down more times than you've got hairs in your moustache.'

Douglas could not resist touching his moustache. After his golf clubs, his job, his degree, his bank-book, his semi-detached villa in Clarkston, and Janet, it was his proudest possession.

'I bet you've been disloyal as often as me, Maxwell.'

That was absurdly unfair. For one thing, Ballantyne was twenty years older, which must have given him many more opportunities. Also Ballantyne was the kind of man who used obscene language in a public dining-room in the presence of ladies, and even worse, who drank two bottles of wine before a golf match. He had no breeding.

Besides, in Douglas's case, were those little adventures with Cissie McDade, Elsie Hamilton, and a few others really acts of disloyalty? Janet would say so, but she was biased. So would David and Mary, but they were religious prudes. So, no doubt, would thousands of other people. But what if they knew all the facts? Remembering Gomez at the airport, he thought enviously of Arab princes. They had dozens of concubines. Their wives probably helped to pick them. Oriental women were wiser in this respect than Western women. They knew that men, especially if they were exceptionally potent, needed more sexual release than any one woman could provide. And what if that one woman for abstruse reasons turned her back on her husband? If

154

she had said she had a headache or it was her period or even that she wasn't in the mood, he would have understood and might even have sympathised; but she baffled him with gibberish about mystery and sacraments. Was he not in such circumstances entitled to appease his natural appetite with other women? Somewhere in the Bible there must be a text granting that entitlement. Had not God ordained that it was a wife's duty to succumb to her husband, preferably in silence? It was one of Douglas's reasons for believing in Him.

4

When Agnes, aged ten, and Jean, aged eight, the one wearing glasses and the other a brace on her teeth, learned that their father was driving out to Ardnave to speak to their Aunt Janet they clamoured to be allowed to go with him. They were fond of Aunt Janet and were anxious to find out how she was getting on in Mr McAllister's house, about which they had heard terrifying tales.

On their father they always used guile: it worked with him but not with their mother. So they gathered some of their oldest picture-books and told him they wanted to give them to the little foreign girl who must be feeling lonely among all the grown-ups at Ardnave.

He was delighted by their thoughtfulness but had to remind them that they must get their mother's permission. They made faces at that, for, like him, they did not think their mother would give it, especially if their father asked for it. He would give in at the first yelled 'No!'

'We'll ask her, Daddy,' said Agnes.

'Well, all right, but don't pester her. She's got a headache.'

The headache had been brought on by the rumpus after lunch. There had been complaints about the language of the Australian, Mr Ballantyne, in the dining-room. Mr and Mrs Donaldson had threatened to leave if he was allowed to stay. Other guests, they said, were of the same mind. The two Misses Cramond, on the other hand, had spoken up in his defence, saying that so robust and virile a man was bound to use robust, virile language. They

157

had found it exhilarating. It was the high spot of their holiday so far.

Mary had a wet cloth over her face. Her daughters took up position in front of her.

Agnes spoke first. 'Mama, Daddy is going to Ardnave to see Aunt Janet.'

'Is that what he told you?'

'We would like to go with him,' said Jean.

'Well, you can't.'

'But it's very nice at Ardnave,' said Agnes. 'Miss McBride told us holy men lived at Ardnave hundreds of years ago.'

'And there are lots of butterflies and sheep and lambs,' said Jean.

That morning Mary had said that McAllister's house should be called Gomorrah.

'Aunt Janet would look after us,' said Agnes.

'Aunt Janet can't look after herself.'

That amazed them. Aunt Janet was the most capable person they knew. They could never take her in as they could Uncle Douglas. They believed utterly in her magical powers of second sight.

'Anyway, Daddy will be with us,' said Agnes.

'Your father can't look after himself either.'

That was true but they loved him for it.

'What's *wrong* with Ardnave?' asked Jean.

'There are foreigners there, from a country where there are terrible diseases, like cholera and malaria. I don't want you catching anything.'

'We'll gargle with Dettol before we go,' said Jean.

'Why do you want to go there anyway? Why aren't you playing with your friends?'

'We want to take some books to the little girl,' said Agnes.

'Doesn't the Bible tell us to be kind to strangers?'

Mary felt a sudden fear. Ought she, in a wicked world, to be discouraging her daughters' Christian instincts?

158

'Would you stay in the car?'

'That would be silly, Mama,' said Agnes.

'It wouldn't be polite,' said Jean.

'You mustn't go into the house.'

'But we'd like to see all the things that Mr McAllister brought from abroad,' said Agnes. 'Miss McBride said it's very educational to see things from other countries.'

'Tell your father I want to see him.'

'Can we go to Ardnave?' asked Jean.

'I want to speak to your father first.'

They rushed away to find him.

A few minutes later he came in, well briefed. They had told him their mother was giving in. He had been warned not to annoy her.

Mary had removed the cloth from her face. She was holding a Bible on her lap.

'Why did you put the idea of going to Ardnave in their heads?'

'I didn't. They were keen to go. They want to make friends with the little girl.'

'Who is this little girl? What's she doing at Ardnave? What's her mother doing? Who is her mother?'

'Janet didn't tell me very much. Mr McAllister knew them in Basah.'

'Just as he *knew* Mrs Ballantyne? All right, I don't want to hear any more about *that*.'

'You see, Mary, Mrs Gomez has come to Flodday to escape from her husband. It seems he has legal authority to take the child from her.'

'I don't wonder he got it, considering the immoral life she seems to have led.'

'But, Mary, the child's been with her mother since she was born. Previously her father wasn't interested in her.'

'But he is now and he's come to get her?'

'He was on the same plane as Douglas. He's staying at Ascog Castle.'

'He must be rich.'

'He's very rich.'

David's heart sank. It had been sinking ever since he had seen the Bible. Mary would think that Gomez had morality on his side, as well as the law, and she had a Biblical respect for wealth.

'All right,' she said, in her grimmest voice.

He didn't understand.

'They can go. Make sure they wash their faces and put on clean dresses.'

5

The girls travelled in the back of the car, for safety. They never sat still or kept quiet. Their interest was in people, not scenery.

'Daddy, why do all the ladies go to stay in Mr McAllister's house?' asked Jean.

'Because they're his friends.'

'Aunt Janet wasn't his friend. She didn't know him.'

'Ronnie McDougall said there are devils in Mr McAllister's house,' said Agnes.

'They won't harm Aunt Janet,' said Jean. 'She's got magic of her own.'

'Is she going to marry Mr McAllister?' asked Agnes.

'Don't be silly, Agnes,' said her father. 'She's already married to Uncle Douglas.'

'But she's fallen out with him.'

'I think Uncle Douglas is better-looking than Mr McAllister,' said Jean. 'Mr McAllister's got a beard. I wouldn't marry a man with a beard.'

'Uncle Douglas has got a moustache,' said Agnes.

'That's not as bad as a beard and he puts scent on it. He wears nicer clothes than Mr McAllister. Doesn't he, Daddy?'

Asked to choose between a navy-blue blazer with gilt buttons and a green corduroy jacket, David played safe and offered no opinion.

'Daddy, was Mr Ballantyne swearing in the dining-room?' asked Agnes.

'He was just talking too loudly, that's all.'

'I heard Mr Donaldson saying that Mr Ballantyne said—' here Agnes stretched forward and whispered into her father's ear – 'c–u–n–t.'

'For heaven's sake, Agnes.'

'Lots of boys at school say that word,' said Jean.

'Some girls too,' added Agnes.

'Well, I hope neither of you say it.'

'Just into ourselves,' said Agnes.

She and her sister laughed. Their father felt flummoxed.

'I like Mr Ballantyne,' said Jean. 'He put his hand on my head and said I reminded him of someone.'

'He's got a daughter in Australia.'

'What's her name?'

'He didn't say.'

'What I don't understand,' said Agnes, unconsciously copying her mother's voice, 'is why Mr Ballantyne and Uncle Douglas went to play golf instead of coming with us to Ardnave.'

'Uncle Douglas said it was a perfect afternoon for golf,' said Jean.

'Well, if one of them was my husband, I wouldn't like it,' said Agnes.

'Can you get a divorce for playing golf?' asked Jean.

'Of course not,' said her father, though he wouldn't have been surprised to be told that golf had been the cause of quite a number of divorces.

'What's the little black girl's name?' asked Agnes.

'She's not black. You two are darker than she is.'

Like all Flodday children they were sunburnt and weather beaten.

'I think she's called Letitia.'

Jean tried to pronounce it but couldn't because of the brace on her teeth. 'What will I call her if I can't say her name?'

'I think it's shortened to Letty.'

'I can say that easily.' She said it three times.

162

'What I don't understand,' said Agnes, 'is why they've come to Flodday? Her and her mother, I mean.'

'Mr McAllister knew them when he was abroad. They've come to visit him.'

'Has Letty's mother got a husband?' asked Jean.

'I think so.'

'Why didn't he come too?'

Her father preferred not to answer that.

'It's very funny Mr McAllister having all the ladies in his house without their husbands,' said Agnes.

'I don't want you two asking nosy questions.'

'Miss McBride said we had to ask to find out,' said Jean.

He was never sure when they were teasing him. They seemed to know more about the ways of the world than he or Mary.

'People don't like being asked nosy questions.'

'Is it because they've got secrets?' asked Jean. 'Mr McPherson told us in Sunday school that nobody should have secrets.'

Agnes corrected her. 'He said that nobody *could* have secrets, because God knew everything.'

She and her sister were amused by the minister's naivety. It didn't matter if God knew your secrets. He could be trusted not to clype.

6

Nell would never forget the shock when she looked out of the kitchen window and saw a tall woman in a blue coat and white skirt and a girl of about ten wearing a white coat, just as Janet had described them in her vision, step out of the car. She had been so utterly convinced that they would not come that when she saw them there she could not believe it. She must be having hallucinations. Janet had infected her. But she was not only seeing them, she was hearing them too. They were talking in a strange language, the woman earnestly, the child peevishly. Nell's own children, tired after a long journey, had been peevish just like this.

She rushed to Angus's studio and banged on the door. 'For God's sake, they've come. She was right after all. She's a bloody witch.'

The door opened. There was a small blob of red paint on Angus's beard, which meant that he must have been painting. She felt glad about that but moments later realised that he was about to receive another severe setback, though perhaps it should have been an inspiration.

'What's the matter?' he asked, peevish himself.

'They've come. God help us, they're out there.'

'Who have come?'

'That woman in your painting upstairs. Though she's got clothes on. A blue coat. There's a kid with her.'

'Fidelia?' He did not know whether to look overjoyed or horrified. What, thought Nell, would make up his mind for him?

They heard the outside door opening and Janet crying joyously. God help her, thought Nell, she thinks he'll be delighted. Where's her second sight now?

They came in, Janet, then Fidelia, and last the little girl.

What Nell noticed first was how the child, though among strangers, did not, as most children would have done, cling to her mother. She kept apart from everyone. Though she held her doll tightly, she was not looking for support from it either. She was on her own. The doll had fair hair and blue eyes, which struck Nell as odd, for its owner's hair was jet-black and her eyes brown.

Throwing away all her reservations, Nell bent down and embraced the little girl. She felt her grow stiff and quickly released her.

Angus and Fidelia were staring at each other.

It seemed to Nell that she was thinner than when Angus had painted her, if, that was, he hadn't in the painting deliberately added on some fat since it had been sexuality he had been after and, like Rubens before him, had not thought it could be done through skinniness.

Not that Fidelia was skinny. For a woman of 36 or so she had a fine figure. In a bikini bottom she would have been whistled at on Bondi Beach, and she would certainly have had the best tan. Her hair was magnificent, jet-black and lustrous. She had the white clean teeth of a fruit-eater.

Nell looked for faults. Were her feet just a bit too big? Her lips too red and thick? Her skin blemished, as if she had had smallpox when a child? Her eyes too meek?

It was her eyes that fascinated Nell most. In their meekness lurked desperation. That was natural, considering the plight she was in. You would see it in a sheep if its lambs were threatened. Yes, but all the sheep could do was stamp its foot and bleat. This tall woman with the blood-red finger nails had savagery stored up in her, for hundreds of years.

166

'Khabar baik, Angus,' she said, in a soft tired voice.

Whatever the greeting meant, Angus responded more like a host than a lover. 'You should have let me know you were coming. I would have met you at the airport.'

You would have made arrangements to be elsewhere. thought Nell. But why the hell am I taking her part against him. I should leave that to Janet.

The child, Nell saw, was beginning to have some trust in Janet, but not yet in Nell, and certainly not in Angus. She made no attempt to hide her dislike of him.

Janet it was who set about making them at home. She took them upstairs, carrying one of their suitcases, and showed them their room. Nell carried up the other suitcase, the heavier one, belonging to Fidelia. They were told where the bathroom was and then left to themselves. Lunch, said Janet, would be in an hour.

As she and Nell went downstairs, Nell grumbled that she had made preparations for three and also that there would be competition for the bathroom, with five people queuing up to use it.

Janet's reply was curt. She would take charge of lunch. Angus could use the monks' privy.

Nell didn't know whether to laugh or be angry. There was no one to tell her either. Thank God she was leaving on Monday.

Janet was taking charge of more than lunch. In the living-room she scolded Angus for his cold reception of Fidelia. 'She's probably breaking her heart.'

Nell doubted it, but did not say so. She remembered Fidelia's eyes.

'What am I to do?' Angus said it twice, once, it seemed, to Buddha.

From the kitchen, where with her sleeves rolled up Janet was already busy, she answered him: 'First of all, we'll have to show

167

her Patel's letter. Then we'll have to persuade her that it wouldn't be safe for her to stay here. Gomez knows about you being here on Flodday.'

'If you think that's what we should do, Janet.'

That whimper Nell interpreted as meaning: 'Nothing would please me more than to get rid of them.' She despised him a bit for his duplicity and cowardice but pitied him too. He just did not have a big enough heart to take on somebody else's troubles and make them his own.

'They'll have to go with Douglas and me on Monday,' said Janet.

Which would leave Angus on his own again. It seemed to Nell he cheered up at the prospect. Probably he saw himself able to return to his painting, with joy and zest.

'Won't Douglas have something to say about that?' asked Nell. 'Pardon me, but you haven't given me the impression that he would welcome into his home strangers with a load of trouble. Few men would.' All the same she knew of one: her Bruce. He would have adopted Angus's child as his own. He would have defied Gomez, for Letty's sake. He had always loved children. No wonder Bruce Junior and Madge had always preferred him. Yes, they had. But she had been a fat slob then, never without a glass in her hand or a fag in her mouth.

'They can stay with us for as long as is necessary,' said Janet.

'How long is that?' asked Nell. 'A month? A year? The rest of their lives? You're not being realistic, Janet.'

'Later I could take them to Skye.'

Nell had to put a brake on her, for all their sakes. 'You've really got nothing to do with it, Janet. Neither have I. It's Angus's business.'

Crouched on the green divan, Angus was staring blankly at Buddha, who was staring blankly back. 'How is it my business?' he whined.

168

'Maybe it isn't. You didn't ask her to come. What was between you is dead and gone. Isn't it?'

'No, it isn't,' said Janet.

'Did they say anything to you in the car?'

'No, they didn't, and I said nothing to them. I thought it better to wait till we were all present.'

'*I* don't particularly want to be present.'

'But you're sorry for them, aren't you?'

'Sure, I'm sorry for them. I'm sorry for millions of people. But, since I can't help them I don't pretend I can.'

'You *can* help Fidelia and Letty. Tell them they'd be safer with me in Glasgow.'

'Would they, though? There would be lots of difficulties you haven't thought of. It might be better if they stayed here with Angus.'

That produced a piteous groan from Angus. He didn't want Fidelia and Letty there but hadn't the guts to say it. He would be ashamed of himself when they were gone, but he would also be very relieved.

Nell gave in. 'All right. I'll say my piece, for what it'll be worth.'

An hour later she volunteered to go upstairs and tell the newcomers that lunch was ready.

She knocked on the door. Little Letty opened it. Beyond her Nell saw Fidelia on her knees in front of the dressing-table which had been turned into a little Catholic shrine. There were little plaster saints, a Madonna in blue, and a picture of Christ with His bleeding heart.

My God, thought Nell, more upset than she had a right to be. If the poor woman thinks praying to these little idols will help, good luck to her.

Letty was gazing up at her. Children were supposed to be more credulous than adults, easily made to believe in angels that protected those who were good and in devils that punished the

169

wicked. Well, here was a ten-year-old face that resolutely rejected all that nonsense. Letty knew that it depended only on people, and in her short life she had learned not to trust many of them.

7

It soon became clear that Letty was not going to be left out of any discussion about her future, and that she would go to bed only when her mother did. So it was decided, by Janet, that Patel's letter should be shown to Fidelia with the child present.

Fidelia read it seated on the green divan, with Letty beside her.

Nell sat on the red divan, though she hated it, for its colour, its lowness, and its inadequate back.

Janet sat on a cushion on the floor, with her legs crossed and her arms folded.

Angus was standing beside Buddha. He seemed to be trying to achieve the same inscrutable smirk.

Nell heard sheep bleating and birds screaming outside. She shut her eyes and remembered Madge when she was ten like Letty. If anyone had tried to take her from her, she would have killed him first.

Letty was now poring over the letter.

Janet broke the silence. 'Do you think you husband will come here?' she asked.

Fidelia nodded. She was in a state of terror.

Letty wasn't, though. She looked pleased. Could she, at her age, understand such a letter? Nell wondered.

'Then you mustn't be here when he comes,' said Janet. 'We don't know if the Scottish courts would recognise his warrants. We'll have to find that out. In the meantime it would be safer if he didn't know where you were.'

Fidelia managed another nod, but Letty shook her head.

Perhaps the kid wants her father to have her, thought Nell. He's rich, isn't he? He's got a house in Forbes Park. God forgive me for thinking that.

'I think,' said Janet, 'and Angus thinks, and Nell too, that you should come to Clarkston with me.'

Janet's in her element, managing other people's lives, thought Nell, and was at once contrite. Never sneer at anyone doing good or trying to do good when you yourself are doing damn-all. The eleventh commandment.

'Tell me what I should do, Angus,' whispered Fidelia.

'I'm afraid Janet's right. If Gomez came here, you'd give in to him, wouldn't you?'

'He is my husband.'

Nell realised then how deep a mess the woman was in. Even God was against her. If Gomez came, God would have brought him and he would have to be obeyed. That she thought she was permitted to try to escape from Gomez, with God's connivance, was contradictory all right, but religion was full of contradictions.

'I understand that,' said Janet. 'If you met him face to face, you'd have to do what he wanted. Yes, I understand that.'

Do you, Janet? asked Nell, inwardly. When you met Douglas face to face, you hit him with a putter. Yet all he'd been doing was a little adultery. A trifle, compared to having your kid grabbed from you.

'But, if you weren't here, that couldn't happen,' said Janet. 'So it's important he doesn't know where you are.'

Nell could have pointed out that if Gomez and his lawyers came to Flodday they would soon find people to sell them information as they had done in Basah. It would be well known in Kildonan that Mrs Gomez and her daughter had left on the Glasgow plane with Mrs Maxwell. After that it would be easy enough to find out where Mrs Maxwell lived.

'On Monday,' said Janet. 'We'll go on Monday.'

Today was Thursday. There was time for Gomez to arrive before Monday.

'It's very kind of you,' said Fidelia.

Was it kindness? Nell supposed so. It would be mean to deny it. But it was also something else. As a child, Janet must have loved to boss her playmates. Here she was at it again. It was a kind of game to her.

Nell wished that she could say something sensible, helpful, and comforting. She couldn't, so she said nothing.

'Letty and I will discuss it,' said Fidelia. 'We will go to bed now. We are very tired. Please excuse us.'

She took Letty's hand, or rather, made to take it. Letty wasn't willing to give it.

When they had gone, there was silence in the living-room.

At last Nell felt she could speak. 'What we haven't taken into consideration is that the kid might want her father.'

'After he's neglected her all her life?' said Janet. 'Don't be ridiculous, Nell.'

'It's not ridiculous.' The voice came from the direction of Buddha. It might have been the god's, so strange it sounded. 'In Basah she told me once that one day she would go to her father.'

'What age was she when she said that?' asked Nell.

'About six or seven. She knew what she was saying. She knows he's rich.'

'That's a disgraceful thing to say, Angus,' said Janet.

'So it is,' said Nell,' but that doesn't mean it's not true. You could see she doesn't want to go to Glasgow with you. She wants to stay here till Gomez comes, till her father comes.'

'Are you saying that she would be prepared to abandon her mother?'

'I expect she's hoping that they'll all be together. Maybe she's got reason for hoping that. We don't know what's passed between Gomez and Fidelia. He may have offered a reconciliation and she turned it down.'

173

'Good for her. According to Angus, he's an evil person, a racketeer. He owns brothels.'

'In Manila that's considered a respectable occupation. Anyway, Angus could be exaggerating. You haven't met him, have you, Angus?'

'Of course not.'

'Well, let's give it a rest for tonight. Even Buddha looks as if he's had enough.'

Next day Fidelia spent a good part of it in her room, praying, Nell was sure, and arguing with Letty or rather being argued with by Letty, in their native language: Tagalog, said Angus. Downstairs they heard Letty screaming. 'She needs her arse spanked,' muttered Nell. Yet all the kid was doing was fighting for her place in the world. Was it possible that in Basah Gomez's lawyers had spoken to the child behind her mother's back? They would have promised glittering bribes. It wasn't that she was a crafty little Filipina. If her skin had been white and her eyes Occidentally blue she would still, in a world she did not trust, have had to show the same stubborn self-interest.

Nell would have liked to speak privately to the child, to try to find out what her hopes and feelings were, and also to show her that people could be trusted. She could not bring herself to do it, though there were opportunities: Letty went for walks by herself, in sight of the house.

Janet had no qualms about interfering. Nell saw her and Letty on the beach. Janet was doing most of the talking.

Later Nell asked her how she had got on with Letty.

'She doesn't say much.'

'Not to us.'

'But I'm sure she wants to do what's best for her mother.'

And for herself, thought Nell. But why expect a child of ten to show them all an example of self-denial?

In Janet's case, whatever it was, it was not self-denial. She was enjoying herself too much. To be fair, she was also greatly relieved. She believed in demons. Every night she asked Angus if he had put out food for them. Nell herself knew that a disaster could be waiting round every corner, but Janet did not just know it, she saw it before it happened, or so she claimed. Had she foreseen one in this house which could only be prevented if Fidelia and Letty were taken away? But if it had been foreseen, surely it must happen.

Angus kept himself locked in his studio, sulking, Nell thought, not painting. She saw him once sneaking back from the monks' privy and waylaid him.

'What do you really want, Angus?'

'What do you mean?'

Outside his own house he looked homeless. Poor Angus.

'What do you want them to do?'

'I don't know.'

'That's not good enough.'

'All right. I think they should go back to Basah.'

'But wouldn't that mean her having to give up Letty?'

'It will come to that in any case.'

'And it doesn't bother you?'

'What bothers me is that I have had to give up my painting.'

'You really are a shit, Angus.'

Yet if Rembrandt, say, had been asked to choose between giving up his painting or betraying a woman he loved, and he had chosen the latter he would have proved himself a good man but the world would have lost many masterpieces. To say that Angus was hardly a Rembrandt would be unfair. There had been a time when Rembrandt was unrecognised.

'You're only giving it up temporarily.'

'I hope so. Otherwise I'll have nothing to live for.'

'Bullshit.'

'What's your own opinion, Nell? You've said very little.'

'They're nothing to me. *I'm* leaving on Monday, whatever

anyone else does. You knew them. You were once in love with Fidelia. You know, I think Janet's right and you're still in love with her. You don't want to be, you hate it as you would a cancer, but it's there, incurable.'

He shook his head.

'All right. I'll tell you what I think. I think you should offer to spend every penny you've got to help her keep her kid. You could also help her to get a divorce and then you could marry her.'

'She doesn't believe in divorce.'

'You said that as if you were glad. I always knew you were no hero, Angus, but I didn't know you were such a shit.' Then she added what afterwards she regretted. 'I'm beginning to think Bruce was right about you.'

On Friday evening after dinner Fidelia announced that she and Letty had decided to accept Janet's offer and go to Glasgow with her. She stared at Angus as she spoke. He stared at Buddha.

Janet was pleased and showed it by kissing Fidelia and giving Letty a hug, which, to Nell's surprise, was not shrugged off. Yet Janet's triumph was subdued, as if she did not want to provoke the demons. Nell herself had almost begun to believe in the damned things. Last night, God help her, she had looked in the shell and been relieved to see bread in it.

'It's a pity there are no boats or planes on Sunday,' said Janet. 'We could have gone then.'

On Saturday afternoon David McNaught arrived with news that changed everything.

8

There was no clubhouse, only a small shed of corrugated iron in which, fastened to the wall by a chain, was a wooden box for the green fees. The money had to be put in through a slot. A typewritten mildewed notice gave local rules: one in particular amused Ballantyne. 'If a ball lands in a cowpat, it may be lifted, cleaned, and dropped, without penalty.' In a bin were some small brooms made of birch twigs. They were for sweeping sheep's droppings off the greens.

Ballantyne was more tolerant than Douglas about these short-comings. It cost a lot of money to keep the grass short; cows and sheep were the cheapest and easiest way of doing it. That was all very well, grumbled Douglas, but they made a mess of the fairways, as did also the myriads of feathers, wild flowers, and mushrooms, which often made the finding of a ball difficult. The greens were protected by barbed wire but sheep still got through and he had once torn an expensive pair of slacks. If it had been a third-rate municipal course, he would not have minded because he never played on such courses. But Flodday was first-rate, potentially as good as any in Scotland.

It annoyed him that Ballantyne was able to be good-humoured and forgiving for a reason that had nothing to do with golf; he was looking forward to seeing his wife that evening. He had already said twice that, whatever the state of the game, they would have to leave no later than six, so that they could get back to the hotel in good time.

Douglas hadn't been able to resist retorting that it was up to

Ballantyne to get a move on, for he, Douglas, was a fast player. In his experience, he had added, Americans and Australians were painfully slow on a golf course. Once, at St Andrews, he had played behind a foursome of Australians, in pouring rain, and the round had taken more than five hours. Their language too had been offensive. They had just been enjoying themselves, said Ballantyne, with a chuckle.

It riled Douglas too that he was still calling Ballantyne by that name, not having been properly sanctioned to call him Bruce, although Ballantyne, without permission, was now calling him Douglas.

Two players were already on the first tee, an old man and his wife, he wearing a cap and plus-fours, she a white hat and long skirt. Both were at least 75. His ball, feebly but cannily struck, travelled no more than a hundred yards but in a straight line. Hers shot sideways into a clump of heather.

She was not discomfited. 'You gentlemen look as if you take the game seriously,' she said, with intended irony. 'Please go ahead.'

'Thank you, ma'am,' said Ballantyne.

Douglas thanked her too but curtly. Incompetent players ought not to be allowed on a golf course. Golf was not a mere game: it was a way of life, a dedication, a religion even.

Douglas won the toss. Taking care not to let anything, even annoyance with Janet, cause him to swing too fast, he performed his usual few twiddles with his driver, necessary for the steadying of his nerves, and then smote the ball. It soared, as did his heart, and flew straight and true for a good 210 yards and, on hitting the fairway, bounded forward another 30 or so, coming to rest in a position from which his second shot to the green would present no difficulty.

'Good shot,' said Ballantyne.

'Bravo,' cried the old man.

'Not bad,' said his wife, who hoped that Ballantyne would hit a better one.

He disappointed her. His ball went further but not so straight, ending up on a high bank amongst marram grass.

He grinned cheerfully and thanked the old couple again.

Then he and Douglas strode off, carrying their bags.

'I don't see how people can enjoy golf if they play it badly,' said Douglas.

'Maybe they were good when they were young.'

'I doubt it.'

'Does your wife play?'

'She tried once but wasn't interested. It's not really a game for women.'

'Nell was always more interested in tennis. But maybe, if all goes well, we could make up a foursome.'

Douglas did not approve of matches arranged for social reasons, where the quality of the golf did not matter.

His ball could not have been lying more conveniently. From past experience he knew in which of the hollows ahead lay the green, and just how far it was. Taking a four-iron, he swung and hit, and had the infinite pleasure of watching his ball fly high and true to its destination. He could not see it land but was confident it was on the green, probably close to the hole. He had an excellent chance of a birdie. He felt exalted, as if he had just proved not merely his skill as a golfer but his worth as a man.

From the high bank Ballantyne had a view of the green and saw where Douglas's ball had come to rest on it. He held his arms apart, to indicate how close to the hole it was.

Douglas's heart always warmed to an opponent sincerely applauding a good shot of his.

Ballantyne could also see the seven-mile long beach, with cattle standing on the white sand. Across the sea-loch white houses shone in the sun. 'Marvellous view from up here,' he cried. Douglas's heart grew warmer still. An opponent who remained cheerful when confronted by superior play was worth beating.

Ballantyne hit the ball delicately for so big a man. It landed on the green but unluckily shot off into a bunker. Nevertheless, it was a meritorious shot and Douglas said so generously. It meant of course that Douglas was going to win the hole.

Tufts of wool clung to the barbed wire. The green was strewn with clusters of black pellets. These Douglas swept away with the broom. They had agreed that he would carry it the first nine holes and Ballantyne the second nine.

Ballantyne in the bunker played his shot. Up came the ball in a shower of sand, landed on the green, and rolled up to the hole, stopping nine inches short. Douglas struck it away with his putter. He knew players who would have made Ballantyne putt it out, but he wasn't mean like that. In any case, Ballantyne's four was soon going to be beaten by his three.

Douglas's own putt was about three feet. He believed in taking his time. He crouched now on this side of the hole and now on that, studying the borrows for a minute at least. Ballantyne stood by patiently. This was commendable. Douglas knew players who fidgeted and mumbled under their breath while he was going through this time-consuming but necessary procedure. At last he was ready. He putted and the ball rolled smoothly into the hole.

'Damned good birdie,' said Ballantyne.

'Not a bad par of your own, Bruce. You don't mind me calling you Bruce?'

'I've been wondering when you were going to.'

They made for the second tee. Douglas felt so friendly and magnanimous that he found himself saying: 'I haven't been quite honest with you, Bruce. You were right in what you said about Janet, my wife. She has run away from me.'

'I wondered why she didn't come to the airport to meet you. I hope it's not serious.'

'No, no. She's a strange girl in some ways. Thinks she has second sight. Born and brought up in Skye. Beautiful, though. You'll see for yourself. Now, Bruce, I'd better warn you about this hole.'

About 50 yards directly in front of the tee was a sandy hillock blocking out all view of the fairway.

'Aim for the middle of the hill,' said Douglas, 'and belt it as hard as you can. It's a long hole and the fairway's pretty wide. High handicappers have trouble getting over the hill. Easy for us, of course.'

He showed how. His ball flew high over the hill.

Ballantyne paused, as he was about to drive. 'You know, Nell must see something in McAllister that I never could.'

A golfer faced with a drive that could go badly wrong ought not to have such matters on his mind. However, they did not put Ballantyne off his stroke. His ball followed Douglas's over the hill.

Douglas was willing enough to chat between shots. He felt close to Ballantyne, who was a good golfer, though not so good as himself. It was a warm sunny afternoon too and the course was in not too bad shape considering: what cowpats there were had dried up, attracting not too many flies. Above all, he, like Ballantyne, had a runaway wife; but his, unlike Ballantyne's, hadn't run away to an old lover. He felt grateful to those McAuslans, whoever they were.

'You may have noticed, Bruce, that I keep myself fit.'

'Yes, I've noticed.'

'Karate as well as golf. Badminton and squash in winter. Women don't seem to appreciate that men who keep themselves in prime condition are bound to have, well, let's be frank, stronger sex urges than men who don't look after their bodies.'

Ballantyne was straight-faced. 'In Basah there were small skinny natives who had more than twenty kids.'

Douglas had a knack of ignoring anything that did not suit his theories. 'Janet's a bit narrow-minded about some things. Her Free Kirk upbringing, I'm afraid.'

'Did she catch you at it bare-arsed?'

181

Though it was to the point, it did not have to be expressed so crudely. Douglas frowned.

They came then to where their balls were likely to have landed. Unfortunately, there were thousands of small white feathers. They began to search.

'This is what I meant,' grumbled Douglas.

'Well, did she?'

'As a matter of fact, she did. A woman I've played golf with. I don't play with many, mind you. We were practising putting on the carpet and having a few drinks. This was in my house. Janet was in Skye visiting her folk. She came back a day sooner than she was expected. Jolly unfair of her, wouldn't you say? Well, Cissie challenged me to this putting match, with our clothes off. She's a good-looking woman, you know. Well, you can guess what followed. We had just finished when Janet came in. I expect it looked suspicious to her. Anyway, she got shirty and hit me with a putter. It was bloody sore. So I lost my temper and gave her a skelp.'

They found their balls. Ballantyne's was about 30 yards ahead of Douglas's. Douglas found it hard to believe that he had been outdriven by a man 20 years older, with a beer-belly too.

'Do you know these people your wife's staying with?' asked Ballantyne.

'No. David said they're called McAuslan. Janet met them through the church. I must say, Bruce, that if she'd gone to somebody like McAllister I don't think I could have taken your broad-minded view.'

'I came here to give him a hiding. I might still do it. But I've got to take into account that he didn't invite her, she invited herself. It could even be that he wasn't all that pleased to see her. The last thing that bastard wants is other people's troubles.'

'These artist types,' said Douglas, 'are poison to women. I read that once.'

9

With so much news to dispense, David did not know how to go about doing it, especially as none of it was really good. Janet would be indignant to hear that Douglas had gone off to play golf, Mrs Ballantyne might well have the same reaction, and Mrs Gomez would be shattered by her husband's arrival.

Luckily Janet and Mrs Ballantyne were by themselves, seated on deck-chairs outside the house. Janet was reading a book, like a harmless holiday-maker. Mrs Ballantyne, alas, was not looking her best. As he soon learned, she had just returned from jogging and was glistening with sweat. She had removed her shorts for coolness and her middle was now covered very inadequately by a black bikini bottom. Tufts of red hair were to be seen and, if anything was to be seen, Jean, and Agnes too in spite of her spectacles, saw it.

There was no sign of McAllister and his other guests.

Jean and Agnes were out of the car before David and made straight for Aunt Janet.

'Where's the foreign girl? We've brought picture-books for her.'

'That's very kind of you. Mrs Ballantyne, these two excited creatures are my nieces, Jean and Agnes.'

'Pleased to meet you, girls,' said Nell.

'Pleased to meet you, Mrs Ballantyne.'

'Letty's gone for a walk with her mother,' said Aunt Janet. 'They won't be long. They went to see the priory ruins and the Cross. Didn't you notice them?'

The ruins were visible from the road.

'No, we didn't. We were too busy talking.'

'Did Mr McAllister go with them?' asked David.

'No. He's in his studio.'

'Can we go and meet them, Daddy?' cried the girls.

'All right.' There would be no danger: the ruins were quite close. Besides, he would be better able to pass on his news if they weren't there, demanding the absolute truth. 'Leave your books here.'

Off they went, skipping and trying to grab butterflies.

'So my adulterous husband did not come after all,' said Janet.

'If you mean Douglas, yes, he did come.'

'Then why isn't he here?'

'He was hurt that you weren't at the airport to meet him.'

'All right. If he wants to keep it up, I don't mind. He's too thick-skinned to be hurt. The only way you could ever hurt Douglas is to accuse him of cheating at golf. Where is he then? Helping at the bar? He fancies himself as mine host.'

'As a matter of fact, he's playing golf.'

It was Mrs Ballantyne who replied. 'I must say that takes the bloody biscuit. He comes to tell his wife he's sorry for giving her a black eye, and what does he do, before he's even seen her? Play golf. Next time, Janet, you should use a driver.'

'Who's he playing with?' asked Janet. 'The local champion? Wherever he goes, he always wants to play the local champion.'

Mrs Ballantyne laughed. 'I used to think my Bruce was bad.'

David coughed. 'He's playing with your husband, Mrs Ballantyne. *He* was on the plane too.'

The effect on Mrs Ballantyne was startling. She let out a wail and looked at herself, her belly, her flushed thighs, her tufts, and her sagging breasts, with disgust. 'My God, he's come to tell me he wants a divorce.'

'I don't think so, Mrs Ballantyne. He wants you to have dinner with him this evening.'

'Candlelight and roses and wine and "How about a divorce, mate?" The sneaky bastard.'

'He wouldn't have come all that way to discuss divorce,' said Janet. 'He'd have waited till you got home.'

'Maybe he couldn't wait. Maybe he's got his chick pregnant.'

David was embarrassed. 'I didn't get that impression, Mrs Ballantyne. He's come because he wants to see you.'

'Bless you for saying so even if it turns out not to be true.'

'Shall I tell him you'll be there tonight? Seven o'clock, he suggested.'

'Christ, yes, wild bulls wouldn't keep me away. Look at me, though. I've given up booze and fags. I don't eat much, I go jogging, and yet I'm still a fat slob. I'm sticky and stinking with sweat, and it's so bloody difficult to get hot water in this house.'

'I'll help you get dressed,' said Janet.

'Douglas wants you to come to dinner too,' said David. He decided not to mention that the winner of the golf match was to pay for the dinners.

'That's a bloody good idea,' cried Nell. 'Come and give me your support and I'll give you mine.'

'What about Fidelia?' asked Janet.

'What d'you mean? You don't think she should be invited too?'

'Why not?'

'Because it's got nothing to do with her.'

'We can't leave her alone with Angus.'

'She won't be alone. She'll have her little watchdog. Anyway she came here to be with Angus. She didn't expect to find us here. If you ask me, she wasn't a bit pleased. She wanted Angus to herself.'

David then had to let drop his third and most shattering bombshell. 'Someone else was on the plane.'

They stared at him in puzzlement.

Nell couldn't help joking. 'The Pope? Mohammed Ali?'

185

'Mr Gomez. He has his lawyer with him.'

'What's going on?' cried Nell. She was really addressing the demons.

Janet had got to her feet. She had a look of dedication that David knew of old and Nell had seen often in the past couple of days. The demons had taken the form of Gomez. Her destiny was to confront and defy him.

They all looked towards the ruins. There was still no sign of Fidelia and the girls.

'Where is he?' asked Janet.

'At Ascog Castle.'

'I had it pointed out to me on the plane,' said Nell. 'It really is a castle. Turrets and all.' The sort of place, she remembered, where the ogres in fairy tales lived. 'They were telling me it costs the earth to stay there.'

'Would you tell Mrs Gomez, Janet, that her husband's come?' said David.

'Yes, after I've been to see him.'

Both David and Nell were put into a state of consternation.

'He'll just tell you to mind your own business,' said Nell, 'Or he'll have you thrown out.' Mind you, she told herself, the saving of a woman and her child from an evil brothel-owner should be everybody's business.

'They'll not let you in,' said David, 'if he says he doesn't want to see you.'

'Which he certainly will say,' said Nell. 'My God, if he came by this morning's plane he could be here any minute. I'll tell you what I'm going to do. I'm going up to have a bath before the place is besieged. I hope you're remembering you've got a date with your husband this evening.'

'This is more important. Will you come with me, David? Don't look so scared. He won't be carrying a gun.'

'I wouldn't bet on it,' said Nell.

'I'll do all the talking.'

'You sure will, even if there's nobody listening. Well, if you do go, God help you, the best of luck. Put a curse on him. Turn him into a rabbit.'

Laughing but shaking her head at the same time Nell picked up her shorts and went towards the house. At the door glancing back she saw that David was trying to keep his eyes off her big fat bulging bum. The monks hadn't been so modest.

Janet was already in the car, in the driving seat. She was not dressed for visiting a hotel that cost £200 per day. Her red dress was becoming but skimpy. Her arms and legs were bare. She wore flip-flop sandals. Her hair was tousled.

They saw Fidelia and the three girls among the ruins. Jean and Agnes were staring at the car, astonished.

Janet stopped the car. 'Tell them we won't be long.'

David put out his head and shouted. 'We'll be back soon. Will you be all right?'

Jean was holding Letty by the hand, determinedly. Letty might not be sure that she wanted this instant and unreserved affection but she was going to get it anyway.

Mrs Gomez looked sad and anxious. Her prayers by the ancient Cross had not lifted her spirits, David thought, but they had made her beautiful, physically and spiritually. It was hardly possible to believe what Janet had told him, that she had head-hunters among her ancestors. No woman could have looked more gentle.

10

Asgog Castle had once been the stately home of Lord Cullipool, whose family had owned a large part of the island. He had sold it and gone to live in Barbados. Now that it was a hotel, it was still as private, sightseers and casual visitors being strictly forbidden. It recruited its guests through an exclusive agency in London, and advertisements in American magazines read by the rich. Minor royalty, British and foreign, patronised it. Its gardens, ablaze with rhododendrons and azaleas in spring and roses in summer, were never open to the public, not even to natives of Flodday. Its tall gates, known locally as the Golden Gates because of their colour, were guarded by a lodge-keeper and two Alsatian dogs. All this secretiveness had given rise to resentful rumours among the locals to the effect that there must be some queer goings-on that they didn't want ordinary folk to know about. No wonder the walls were blushing, this being a reference to the virginia creeper with which they were covered. It was certainly the case that rich elderly ladies sometimes arrived at the airport escorted by men too young, vigorous, and cocky to be their husbands, and also rich elderly gentlemen with women in tow too amorous-looking to be their wives and too brazen-looking to be their daughters.

David did not think they would be allowed past the gates. They would be taken for nosy holiday-makers. Notices abounded warning off such nuisances.

Beside him Janet's mouth was tight and her eyes fey. God knew what she intended to say to Gomez if she saw him. Luckily, that wasn't likely.

He kept expecting the hotel limousine to pass them, going the other way. In the back would be two dark-faced men.

Janet drove boldly up to the gates and tooted her horn.

The two big dogs came bounding and barking, soon to be followed by the lodge-keeper, a small bald dignified man in a black uniform. He was putting on a black cap with the hotel's name on it.

Janet got out and went up to speak to him.

'What d'you want?' he asked. 'Can't you read?'

He knew she wasn't a guest. For one thing, people didn't just take a whim to stay at Ascog Castle: they had to be vetted first, in that office in London. Being rich wasn't enough. Football pools winners, for instance, stood no chance of being accepted. For another thing, nobody arriving in a car like that could afford the prices.

'I've come to see Mr Gomez,' she said. 'He's a guest here. He arrived this morning.'

'Did he now?' But her information was correct. Mr Gomez *had* arrived that morning, with his lawyer. The story was that he had come to buy an estate on the island. He had smelled sweeter than any man should but his tip had been manly enough. He had said little, leaving the talking to the lawyer. Rich people were usually like that, they hadn't much to say. Perhaps it was because they were too busy counting their money in their heads. Jock Scobie could toady as adeptly as any flunkey in Buckingham Palace but inwardly he sang a different tune, having been born in Glasgow.

Guests, especially Mafia types like Gomez, brought their trollops with them. Was this his just arriving? She looked fierce, like a tinker wife. He'd have to be careful she didn't lib him with her teeth, as shepherds did lambs. The furtive fellow in the car must be her pimp. Well, there were all sorts of ways of making a living.

'I'll have to check that,' he said. 'People come to the gate and

190

tell a pack of lies. They just want to see round the place. But that's not permitted. Guests here pay salt for their privacy. What name will I say?'

'Tell him I'm from Mr McAllister. It's about Fidelia.'

'Fidelia?' There was disbelief in his voice. Yet he kept calling his dogs Hector and Achilles.

'He'll know who I mean.'

He went off to telephone.

Janet talked to the dogs. They growled back.

The lodge-keeper returned and opened the gates. 'Ask at the desk,' he said.

'Thank you.'

The quarter-mile drive to the hotel was through parkland. This was the most sheltered part of the island. Trees of all kinds grew here, including palms. Near the hotel were masses of roses. The air was fragrant with them.

The chips of gravel were white as snowberries: it was said they had been brought from Italy. On either side of the door was a large statue, also of marble, one of a naked woman with a finger coyly at her chin, and the other of a naked man with no fig leaf.

A butterfly fluttering past was bigger, more dainty, and more pleased with itself than the butterflies in the streets of Kildonan.

Coming out of the front door was a woman of at least 60, dressed in pink, on the arm of a tall black-haired young man wearing a striped blazer and tight white trousers. His smile was not that of a son, nor was hers that of a mother.

'So it's true,' said Janet.

'He could be her nurse.'

'He could be King Kong.'

Janet was wishing that Douglas was with her. No one was more firmly established in the real world than he. Because he lacked imagination, he was never ill at ease whatever the place or company. He would not have been intimidated by Gomez's wealth and reputation. On the contrary, he would have felt

191

superior because he was white, with all of Western civilisation behind him: an impudence considering his opinion of artists and his taste in books, which was restricted to thrillers and golf magazines.

'Have you changed your mind?' asked David, as she hesitated.

'No, I haven't.'

She got out of the car and went boldly into the hotel.

The hall was vast. In it were suits of armour and sombre paintings. The reception desk was attended by a pasty-faced clerk in a dinner jacket. One glance told him she wasn't a guest; all his subsequent glances were lewd and sly.

'Mr Gomez is expecting me,' she said.

'Señor Gomez?'

He would never have leered at Douglas like that. He might have sniggered behind Douglas's back, but to his face he would have been respectful.

'If you would be so good as to wait in the lounge.' Then he added, in a whisper: 'I'm off duty in an hour, duckie. What about it?'

Evidently he was accustomed to getting for free what the guests paid large sums for.

She let Nell answer for her: 'Go to hell.'

On her way to the lounge she passed a white-haired man taking the arm of a girl who could have been his granddaughter, but wasn't.

There was only one person in the huge lounge: an old man snoozing noisily. At £200 a day those were expensive snores.

She sat in a corner by a window that looked out on to rosebeds. The size and splendour of the room would have impressed Douglas but he would not have been awed. He would instead have looked for the bell to summon a waiter. Only when he had given his order and so asserted his right to be there would he have admired, briskly, the high corniced painted ceiling, the enormous black fireplace, the silver rose-bowls, the thick carpet, and the frames of the pictures. But it would have been his holding his own with anyone else there, even if they were millionaires, that would have been his main concern.

She thought of Gomez's two million-dollar house in Manila, in the residential area with the Scottish name, Forbes Park. There would be a room in it as magnificent as this, and ornaments as beautiful and valuable. Would there be indications that he was a Catholic, a friend of bishops, according to Angus? Holy pictures? Gold crucifixes?

She remembered Fidelia's little shrine.

She looked round. A man had come into the room, dark-faced, but he wasn't Gomez. The lawyer, no doubt. He came over to her, smiling courteously. He should have been leering evilly.

She stood up, again wishing that Douglas was with her. She felt like a character in a fairy tale whose magical powers had suddenly left her. Turn him into a rabbit, Nell had said. She could not prevent this grey-haired man from looking like a kindly grandfather.

'I don't think you gave your name,' he said. He had an American accent.

'Janet Maxwell.'

'Please sit down, Miss Maxwell. I understand that you have come from Mr McAllister?'

'Yes.'

'How very convenient. We were about to despatch a messenger to Mr McAllister. It seems he is not available by telephone. You can convey the message, if you would be so kind.'

'I came to see Mr Gomez.'

'I'm afraid that is not possible. I am Señor Garcia, Señor Gomez's lawyer. He has asked me to speak to you on his behalf. Here is the message. Would you please inform Mr McAllister and the lady who is with him that Señor Gomez and I will have the pleasure and honour of calling on them tomorrow at eleven o'clock.'

'What do you intend to do? Why have you come to Flodday?'

'It will be explained tomorrow. Good afternoon, Miss Maxwell. Thank you for calling.'

He gave a little bow, looked as if he might have kissed her hand, and then made for the door. Passing the old man asleep in the armchair he walked ever so quietly. Such consideration, she thought bitterly.

She was not so sure now that she would have the resolution to oppose Gomez. The demons were on his side.

She did not know whether to be comforted or exasperated by David's face, familiar, concerned, and sympathetic, but destitute of any magical power. Never before had she felt so held back by human limitations, her own as well as his. He had moved into the driving seat. How could he help her to challenge and overcome a Manila racketeer when he was scared of fast driving?

'You weren't long,' he said. 'How did you get on. What's he like?'

'I didn't see him. He sent his lawyer. They're calling on Angus and Fidelia tomorrow at eleven.'

'We'll all be in church then.'

She felt like screaming. Yet how could he have said, in a land of Christians, anything more relevant?

'Do you know anyone with a boat big enough to take us to the mainland?' she asked.

They stopped at the gates. The lodge-keeper came out and opened them. He waved them through. Hector and Achilles barked farewell.

'Dugald McAskill sometimes takes parties to the mainland,' said David.

'Good. Where does he live?'

'In Ballaigmore. But he was taking the shinty team to Pabbay this afternoon.' Pabbay was an adjacent island. 'They won't be home till late.'

'It doesn't matter how late. Even if it was after midnight. It's

194

never really dark at this time of year. We've got to get Fidelia and Letty away before tomorrow morning.'

'They'll not be sober, either. The shinty team, I mean. Dugald won't do it, Janet.'

'Tomorrow morning then.'

'It's the Sabbath. He'll not take his boat out on the Sabbath.'

'Is there anyone who will?'

'No.'

'Then we'll have have to hide them.'

'Where?'

'Anywhere. A cave would do.'

'You're being silly.'

To their left then, in the distance, was the golf course. They could see red flags. They saw golfers too but could not tell if Douglas and Mr Ballantyne were among them.

'I can't help feeling sorry for Mr McAllister,' said David. 'Just a few days ago he had no worries except how to improve his painting.'

'Well, all this should make him a better painter or make him give it up altogether.'

They stopped outside the hotel. David got out. Janet moved over.

'I'll bring Jean and Agnes back about seven.'

'Have I to tell Douglas that you'll be having dinner with him?'

'Yes. You can warn him.'

'Will you be staying the night here?'

'I don't know that yet. See you later.'

11

The measure of how much Douglas had come to like and respect his opponent could be judged by his raising only the mildest of objections when, on the seventeenth tee, with the game even, Ballantyne looked at his wrist-watch and cried, 'My God, it's twenty past six. I'd better get back to the hotel.' As he hurried away towards the hired car, with Douglas pursuing him, he said that they might be able to play the last hole tomorrow, and another round as well, if the ladies were agreeable.

He was forgetting that golf was not allowed on Flodday on Sundays.

It would be the second arrangement to which the ladies were to be asked to agree. Douglas had offered to conduct Ballantyne on a tour of some famous Scottish courses. He was due a few days off work. They could leave Flodday by the plane on Monday and from Glasgow Airport take a taxi to Douglas's house in Clarkston, where they could pick up the Rover and be on their way to Troon by two. They could then play the Old Course. Thereafter they could either spend the night on the Ayrshire coast and play Turnberry next day or they could return to Clarkston and proceed from there to St Andrews. Then they could head for Gleneagles. It would be hectic and expensive but well worth it. If the ladies wanted to come along for the ride, they would be welcome; if not they could entertain themselves in Glasgow.

Enthusiastic as a golfer, Ballantyne had been cautious as a husband. It would depend on Nell. This had struck Douglas as odd because, after all, Mrs Ballantyne, like Janet, was the guilty

197

party, having run away, and, unlike Janet, was at present living with a former lover, a lecherous creep of an artist. By all the rules of the game, her permission ought not to have been necessary.

On the way back to the hotel Douglas reviewed his own attitude to Janet. Perhaps it would be too harsh, not to say imprudent, if he was to demand an apology and an undertaking never to leave him in the lurch again. A few signs of repentance on her part might be enough.

He decided to wear his kilt that evening. It would be in honour of Bruce and Mrs Ballantyne but it would also be a signal to Janet that, as far as he was concerned, hostilities were over. She was proud of him in a kilt. Few men in Scotland wore it better.

Luckily, David was doing a stint behind the bar, so that they could learn from him whether or not their wives were coming to dinner and at the same time order refreshing pints. Yes, they were coming, he said. Ballantyne gladly left it at that but Douglas wanted to know more about the McAuslans, Janet's hosts. He would like to meet them and thank them for being hospitable to his wife.

In his softest voice David assured him that that the McAuslans seldom came into Kildonan, except, of course, to go to church. Who were they? Well, Mr McAuslan had been a civil servant in Glasgow. He had retired to Flodday to study birds. Mrs McAuslan did a little painting. That one on the wall, of Clachaig Bridge, was by her. On his way over to Ballantyne, Douglas paused, a glass of beer in each hand, to admire Mrs McAuslan's work. He thought it was very good. The price, though, was steep. For £50 you could buy four dozen Dunlop 65s.

Before he had drunk a quarter of his pint, Ballantyne had finished his and was off upstairs to prepare for his wife's coming. He was as eager, Douglas jested to David, as a youth in love for the first time. Yet hadn't Mary said that Mrs Ballantyne was fat? It went to show that even the toughest of men, the fastest beer drinkers, and the most filthy-tongued, could be mushy where women were concerned.

198

12

When Janet got back to Ardnave, her nieces were having a great time in Letty's room trying on her dresses and taking turns of nursing her doll. Nell, having bathed, was lying on her bed with her eyes closed, hoping, she said, when Janet looked in, that when she opened them she would see in the mirror opposite a slim, elegant, desirable, beautiful lady. Did Janet have a really seductive scent? No, she didn't think Janet would have. Fidelia might, though. Only then did she remember to ask how Janet had got on. She wasn't surprised nor much interested when Janet told her that Gomez and his lawyer were coming to Angus's on Sunday morning. She said she hoped Bruce had ordered a room with a double bed. No, she hadn't mentioned to Angus or Fidelia that Gomez had arrived on the island. She had left that to Janet.

Downstairs Janet found that Angus had at last crept out of his studio. He was having a conversation in the living-room with Fidelia, or rather, he was listening, remote as Buddha, while Fidelia quietly and passionately pleaded with him.

When Janet came in, he made to get up, but she asked him to stay. She had something to say to Fidelia which affected him too. She sat on the green divan. Angus was occupying the red, Fidelia the yellow.

They could hear the children's screams of happiness overhead.

'I believe Mr Ballantyne came on the plane today,' said Angus, with a sneer. 'An event you failed to foresee.'

'Someone else was on the plane,' she said. 'I failed to foresee that too. Your husband, Fidelia. He has a lawyer with him.'

She could have sworn that for a few seconds Angus looked quite gleeful. Thereafter, he frowned and tried to look sad.

Fidelia was silent. She sat upright, a feat on those divans. Her heart must have been racing with fear but her hands on her lap were still. Surely no man in the world could have rejected so lovely, so intelligent, and so brave a woman. There were two, Angus and Gomez; but perhaps they were all being premature in assuming that Gomez had come only for Letty. How marvellous if, at Ardnave, with its lambs and larks and monks' ghosts, the Gomez family was united.

Fidelia must have had some such hope, for, when Janet suggested that she and Letty should go into hiding somewhere until Gomez had gone, she shook her head. She would discuss it with Letty, she said. Then she turned to Angus and asked him what they should do.

What answer did she expect? That when Gomez came, he, Angus, would never allow them to take Letty? That he would snatch the warrants out of their hands and tear them up? That he would himself hire lawyers and fight the case for years if need be until Letty was of age and that, in the meantime, they were welcome to live in his house for as long as they wished?

What he did say was: 'How should I know?'

In Fidelia's place, Janet would have hit him. There was no putter handy but, within reach, Fidelia had a choice of a small statue of Ganesh, the elephant god, or a Buddha of green soapstone, either of which would have made a formidable missile.

Fidelia had no violence in her. She rose, smiled at Janet, looked sadly at Angus, and went out. Janet heard her opening the outside door and then saw her through the window making her way slowly towards the beach. Surely she wasn't thinking of drowning herself? No, as a Catholic she would never do that. Besides, the tide was well out. She would have had to walk for half a mile to reach drowning depths.

What she was doing was preparing herself for a sacrifice more painful than being burned to death, and it would last for the rest of her life. In her room she had some religious books. Without permission Janet had looked through them. One was about the torments of hell. There were illustrations. One showed a naked woman with tiny sharp-toothed devils nibbling at her toes, her private parts, her breasts, and her face. How in God's name, Janet had wondered, can she look so calm with such horrors in her mind?

Janet turned on Angus, who was nibbling at his knuckles. 'You ought to know,' she said, scornfully, 'if you love her. She came to you for help. You've given her none.'

'All I want is to be left alone to get on with my painting. That's all I've ever wanted. Why can't you all leave me alone?'

'You use people, Angus. They don't like being used and then thrown away like paper hankies.'

'An artist has to use people. Writers too. They know it's despicable sometimes but, if they don't do it, they won't learn and, if they don't learn, they can't paint or write and there would be no masterpieces.'

'So we're all just material to you?'

'Yes. Yes. Yes.'

'You'd have to be as good as Picasso to get away with that.'

'No. Even the worst of us.'

'So when Gomez comes tomorrow and demands that Letty be handed over to him, you'll just stand by and let it happen?'

'She's the one who'll let it happen. She's known since Letty was born that it would happen one day. You see, she's got to obey God.'

'So God wants her to give her daughter to a man that owns brothels?'

'I don't know what God wants. She thinks she does. I don't even know that God exists.'

'Tell me this, Angus. Let's suppose that Letty's been taken

from her, would you let her stay here with you, would you be kind to her, would you help her to get over it?'

He was silent. She hated him for it and yet he was being honest. He could have lied.

She looked at the time. It was almost six o'clock. She would have to go and get dressed. It was suddenly important to her not to let Douglas down.

13

David was in the bar when, just after seven, the car arrived bringing Janet, Nell, and his two girls. Sadie the maid came in to tell him. He had arranged for her to take over for half an hour. He had to have a word in private with Janet before she spoke to Douglas, who was in his room getting dressed. Fortunately, putting on a kilt was for him a lengthy ceremony.

He found Jean and Agnes in the kitchen telling their mother about the wonderful time they had had. They showed the presents Letty had given them: small animals carved out of wood, in Jean's case a sad-eyed monkey, and in Agnes's a long-legged bird. They were begging their mother to let Letty come and play with them tomorrow. Daddy or Aunt Janet could go and fetch her. When Mary reminded them that tomorrow was Sunday and they had church and Sunday school to attend, they cried that didn't matter, Letty could go with them, she was a Christian, she had a wee gold crucifix round her neck. They uttered strange words. 'Emak.' That was Malay for mother. 'Bapa.' That was Malay for father. Mary was touched that those were the words their new friend had taught them.

David took his daughters to the private sitting-room. They had just got there when there was a knock at the door. It was Janet, accompanied by Mrs Ballantyne.

David was glad to see Mrs Ballantyne looking so eager and attractive. He would not have called her fat. Well-upholstered, his father would have said. He did not know it but it was thanks to her girdle, worn with heroic fortitude. Her green dress suited her. Over her red hair was a gauzy scarf embroidered with butterflies in bright colours. Fidelia had lent it to her.

'Your husband's in the lounge bar,' he said. 'Shall I go and tell him you're here?'

He thought they might want their reunion to be private.

'No. That's all right. We like company. Wish me luck.'

They wished her luck.

'She won't need it,' said David. 'He's on edge waiting for her.'

'Waiting to tell her he wants a divorce?'

'Waiting to tell her how much he's missed her.'

'I hope so. Well, what about my own beloved. Is he missing me?'

He glanced at his daughters, resting after the day's excitements. 'Let's go to my office, Janet.'

She was wearing a white blouse cut so low at the neck that part of her bosom could be seen. Douglas would not be pleased. This shamelessness was emphasised by a jade necklace which David had never seen before. It had been lent by Fidelia.

In the office, David looked at his cousin across the desk, past the penguin.

'You're looking like Bonzo again,' she said.

'It's that blouse, Janet. Douglas won't like it.'

'I can assure you Cissie McDade was showing a lot more than this.'

He sighed. 'I've been worried about Mrs Gomez. Jean and Agnes seemed to have enjoyed meeting the little girl. What do you think's going to happen?'

'I don't know. Maybe she's hoping for a miracle.'

As well as the book about the torments of hell, Fidelia had one about miracles.

'Did you mention about them hiding somewhere? I've been thinking about that.'

'She's refused. She wants to go through with it. She seems resigned. Angus is a beast.'

'Why, what has he done?'

'It's what he hasn't done and has no intention of doing. Helping her, giving her support. He says it's none of his business. All he wants is to get on with his painting.'

'I see.' What David saw was that McAllister deserved as much to be pitied as blamed.

'Well, is my darling in the lounge bar too?'

'No. He's upstairs dressing. He's wearing his kilt, in your honour he says.'

'He's wearing a kilt because he wants to show off to Nell. What sort of man is Mr Ballantyne?'

'I'm afraid he caused a bit of a scandal at lunch with his bad language. There were complaints. But the children like him. So does Douglas.'

'Douglas must have beaten him then. He likes people he beats. He's not so fond of those who beat him.'

'That's not fair, Janet. It was a draw. They had to stop at the seventeenth. They ran out of time. There's something I'd better tell you, Janet.'

'About my adulterous husband?'

David winced. 'You see, Janet, I didn't like to tell him you were staying with Mr McAllister. He might not have understood. So I'm afraid I made up a story that you were staying at Ardnave with a family called McAuslan.'

'McAuslan? Remember the wee minister in Portree called that? He had a wig that kept coming loose in the pulpit. But, David, there are no people called McAuslan living at Ardnave.'

'I know that. I invented them.'

She laughed. She had invented a lot of people in her day. This was David's first time. 'Good for you. Tell me about them. In case he asks.'

'Well, you met them in church.'

'What a liar you are, David McNaught!'

'Mr McAuslan is a retired civil servant from Glasgow. He

205

came to Flodday to study birds. Mrs McAuslan is an artist. She's got paintings on the wall in the lounge bar.'

'Those are Miss Sievewright's.'

'I know that.'

'Well, I suppose he'd have to stand on a chair to read the signature. Have the McAuslans got white hair? Do they like malt whisky? Have they got a daughter in New Zealand?'

David smiled weakly. 'I had to tell Mary.'

'You mean to say that Mary agreed to tell lies? What would Mr McPherson say?'

'He's not saying very much these days. People are wondering if he's ill.'

'To get back to Mary, she didn't repeat all those lies to Douglas, did she?'

'No. She didn't give me away, that's all. She thought your marriage was in danger. She likes Douglas.'

'Knowing him to be an adulterer? But then, as we discovered in Sunday school, so was King David. What's keeping him? Can't he get his kilt to hang straight?'

'How did Mr McAllister take the news that Gomez is to visit him tomorrow?'

'As my mother would say, his face is tripping him.'

But what man McAllister's predicament would not be long-faced?

There was then a bang on the door and in marched Douglas, kilt swinging. David made an excuse and fled.

Douglas, exuding forgiveness, made to kiss her. She pushed him away.

He noticed her blouse. 'I say, isn't that a bit risqué? It might do in sophisticated circles but not here among the heather-loupers.'

'You weren't so concerned about Cissie McDade's lack of modesty.'

'For God's sake, Janet, why bring that up? Let's be adult about it. You forgive me, I forgive you. That's all there is to it.'

'What am I to be forgiven for?'

'Well, you did hit me with the putter. It was jolly sore. And you did run away. Let's call it quits.'

'How do I know that, while you were on your own, there wasn't someone else? Elsie Hamilton, for instance.'

'Good heavens, you'd think I was a regular Casanova to hear you. How did Rabbie put it? [Douglas had attended many Burns Suppers at the golf club.] Every man gangs a kenning wrang. Look at the number of times Jean Armour had to forgive him.'

'More fool she. And I'm not married to Robert Burns.'

Douglas decided to change the subject. 'Where's Mrs Ballantyne?'

'In the lounge bar, being reunited with her husband.'

'By Jove, wasn't he boiling over to see her again.'

'Was he?'

'Could hardly play golf for talking about her. Came dashing off the course in case he would be late. I never saw anything like it.'

'She was just as keen to see him. There's a joyful reunion going on in the lounge bar. Let's go and congratulate them.'

'Just a minute. Tell me about these McAuslans you were staying with.'

'Why? Are you suspicious?'

His astonishment was genuine. 'Why should I be suspicious?'

'I thought you might be thinking that David made them up.'

'Made them up? What are you talking about?'

'He did make them up. Invented them. To protect me. From your jealous wrath. You see, I was staying with Angus McAllister.'

Douglas was having difficulty taking it in. 'McAllister? The fellow Mrs Ballantyne was staying with?'

'That's him.'

'A painter?'

'Yes.'

'The two of you?'

She could have said the three of us, but he was astounded enough.

'What have you and this creep McAllister been up to?' he howled.

'Make less noise. What if I were to say, the same thing you and Cissie were up to on my Afghan rug?'

'You know it's different for a woman.'

He knew it sounded feeble but he believed it and was sure that somewhere in the Bible were texts supporting him.

'How is it different?'

'A woman could become pregnant.'

'A man could become a father.'

'Yes, but he wouldn't know it, the way a woman was bound to. Apart, altogether, from the morality of the thing, a woman's got to be more careful than a man. That's the way nature arranged it.'

'That might have been the case before the Pill was invented. Women can now have the fun without the consequences, just like men. That's only fair, wouldn't you say? As a golfer, you must see that.'

He looked so guilty and miserable that she almost relented. She was not to know that he was thinking not of Cissie, but of Elsie.

'We'll finish this talk later,' she said. 'How did you get on with Nell's husband?'

'All right. He's a bit uncouth. Uses indecent language in the presence of ladies. But he's an Australian, of course.'

'At least he doesn't expect his wife to be faithful to him when he isn't faithful to her.'

'That blouse, Janet. Couldn't you pin it up a bit?'

'Why? Are you ashamed of your wife's bosom?'

'They'll ogle. You didn't, did you, with McAllister? The bloody nerve of the man, two women in his house at once.' That was an indignant squeal, with traces of envy.

'Three,' she said, unable to resist. 'Let's go and join them.'

As she passed him, she placed in his open mouth a feather plucked from the penguin.

14

As she entered the lounge bar Nell was holding her breath, not only because of the tightness of her girdle: suspended joy was just as constricting. She tried to carry herself with elegance: something else borrowed from Fidelia. The place was crowded, so that it took her a few seconds to find Bruce in a corner. A cheerfully insolent, normally salacious young man with long hair greeted her with a whistle of admiration, which his two cronies echoed. (They were the three who last Saturday had baited Angus McAllister.) Bruce glanced up to see what specimen of female bedworthiness had evoked these salutes. When he saw her, his face, a moment ago downcast, lit up. Years of stale custom dropped off it. She saw him as he had been on their honeymoon, when she had taken the photograph of him as Atlas. He came rushing over with such unguarded delight that the youths, ready to mock middle-aged or elderly love, instead gave their ironical but good-natured blessing. Nell, inwardly calling them cheeky young buggers, was grateful. It was reassuring to learn from such prejudiced critics that her own and Janet's efforts, with shy assistance from Fidelia, to disguise the puffiness of her face and put the sheen back in her hair, had been successful.

The world, she felt, was a happy place, full of good well-intentioned people. Bastards like Gomez were few and they wouldn't win in the end. Later, when her happiness was at its height, remembering Fidelia, she would not be so confident of the triumph of the innocent.

She and Bruce had never made a habit of slobbering over each other in public. They did hold hands, though.

'Pleased to see you, sport,' said Nell.

'Me too. You look marvellous.'

'I feel marvellous. You don't look so bad yourself.'

He took her to a seat. 'What would you like to drink?'

'I'm going to tell you something that'll make your jaw drop. I've given it up.'

'Given what up?'

'Booze. Fags too. I'm a reformed character.'

'Have you joined a nunnery?'

'No. I've still got one wicked habit left, as you'll find out later. I'll have a glass of lemonade. But, since this is a special occasion, I'll have some whisky in it. Flodday Mist. The local champagne.'

'Right. Flodday Mist and lemonade. That's a handsome scarf. I haven't seen it before.'

'It's not mine. I borrowed it.'

'From Janet?'

'No. I'll tell you about it later.'

He went off to fetch her drink. Sadie was still behind the bar.

Nell might have been a nun, so solemnly did she look about her. She could not resist giving the randy youths a wink.

Bruce came back. His tie, as always, was askew. She straightened it and then patted his cheek. 'Here's to us,' she said, lifting her glass.

'To us, Nell.'

'The bridge is still standing.'

All their married life, in the midst of crises, such as when both the children had whooping cough, it had been their custom to cheer each other up by pointing out that Sydney Harbour Bridge was still standing and so there was no need to despair.

'It sure is. You're looking a treat, Nell. Fair blooming. The pure air of this place must suit you.'

'You should have seen me yesterday. I've had a bit of good

news since then. I'm a new-born woman. I know now how those buggers feel when they say they've found God. So what did you think of Janet's Douglas?'

Bruce grinned. 'He's all right, I guess. A bit bumptious. Too full of himself. Needs sorting out. Not a bad golfer.'

'Did you beat him?'

'We were all square at the seventeenth. I packed it in then, so as not to be late.'

'Was he willing to pack it in?'

'To him it was like leaving the church before the service was finished.'

'You used to be like that yourself.'

'I've learned sense.'

'So will he. Janet will sort him out, no bother.'

'What's she like?'

'Ah well, now, that would take some answering. When I was a kid, I had a Bible with coloured pictures. One was of Jephthah's daughter. That's all she was called: Jephthah's daughter.'

'Never heard of her. But then, I didn't have your religious upbringing.'

She smiled. 'Well, Jephthah was a mighty man in Israel. He won a battle with the Lord's help and, to show his gratitude, he made a vow that he would offer as a sacrifice to the Lord the first person he saw coming out of his house when he got back home. Well, out ran his daughter to welcome him. He was heart-broken. She was his only child, you see, and he loved her very much. But he'd given his word to the Lord and – this is the bit that reminds me of Janet – she insisted that he keep it. So she was sacrificed. The picture was of her being prepared for it by her maidens.'

'Was she burned to death or did the priest cut her throat?'

'I don't think it says. That's Janet. She'd like to be a sacrifice if she could find a cause good enough. Black hair, pale face, tight lips, mad eyes.'

211

'I can't see Douglas coping with a woman like that.'

'Not many men could. She's a rum lady is Janet. Climbs clifs that would frighten a goat. Crawls into a cave as black as hell, with not so much as a match. Thinks she's got second sight and it's possible she has. Pokes her nose into everybody's business. She's got herself mixed up in something that could turn out nasty but I'll tell you about it later.'

'Who are these people she was staying with?'

'What people?'

'Called McAuslan.'

'Who told you that?'

'David. Her cousin. The guy that owns this hotel.'

'He was kidding you. I expect he didn't want Douglas to know she was staying with Angus. Like me.'

This was dangerous ground.

'Angus being McAllister?'

'That's right. Her, me, and another dame. I'll tell you about her later. This is her scarf. Here they come at last. My God, he's wearing a kilt.'

'She doesn't look so fierce.'

Janet was smiling graciously. Like Jephthah's daughter, thought Nell, feeling uneasy.

'You didn't say she was a fine-looking woman,' said Bruce.

'Keep your eyes off her books.'

But he didn't and no other man in the bar lounge did either.

The three youths, Donald, Dugald, and Torry, had been told that the conceited character in the kilt was the mysterious ex-barmaid's husband. They jested lewdly as to whether under that bright tartan sulked a cock with bits bitten off it.

Janet and Douglas went over to their friends.

'Bruce, meet Janet,' said Nell. 'Janet, meet Bruce.'

Nell could see that Bruce, a sensitive big bugger though he didn't look it, was immediately aware of Janet's rumness and found it fascinating.

Janet, for her part, was gracious to him, like a princess to a well-meaning lout.

Nell took note, grimly.

Introducing Douglas, Janet was indulgent. If he's a buffoon, her smile said, don't hold it against him, he can't help it. Admire, please, his kilt, see how straight his sporran is hanging, and isn't his moustache cute?

Evidently he had not apologised satisfactorily for the hanky-panky on the Afghan rug. Nell rather liked him. He thought so highly of himself that he didn't give a damn what other people thought of him. And why not?

'What are you two drinking?' asked Bruce.

'Thank you, Bruce,' said Janet. 'Flodday Mist with a little water, please.'

Douglas pretended to find that funny. 'When did you start drinking whisky?' he asked. And what other vices did you pick up in McAllister's house, his tone implied.

'This very minute,' said Janet, smiling sweetly. 'To celebrate this happy occasion.'

'All right.' He couldn't help making it sound as if he was giving his permission. 'I'll have the same, Bruce, if you don't mind.'

At the bar Bruce had a word with David, now behind it.

'These McAuslans,' he whispered, 'are they here?'

'They don't drink,' murmured David.

Bruce laughed. 'You've been rumbled, though. Douglas knows.'

'Yes. Janet told him.'

'Mind you, I don't think the lady needs anybody's help.'

'That's not so, Mr Ballantyne. She's very highly strung. You see, she has pyschic powers. She sees things happening before they do. An aunt of hers, who was like that, went mad. Her family have always been anxious about Janet.'

'Is that so? I didn't know. I'm sorry to hear it.' But why an

213

God's name would a woman like that marry a man like Douglas, with no more imagination than a golf ball?

'Will you be ready for dinner soon?' asked David. 'We have prepared a private room for you.'

'That's kind of you.' Was it so that there would be no cursing to offend the other guests? Or was it in case Janet, as the Yanks say, blew her top?

He went back with the drinks on a tray.

'Our host says we're to have dinner in a private room. He wants us to go there shortly.'

'I'd like to drink a toast first,' said Nell.' Will you join me, Bruce, in drinking a toast to Janet and Douglas?'

'With pleasure.'

'May they have a dozen kids.'

Douglas laughed. 'Three more and we could have a rugger team. But thanks all the same. Janet, let's drink to Nell and Bruce. May they be as happy for the rest of their lives as they are now.'

He end Janet clinked glasses and drank the toast.

It seemed to Bruce that a weird look had come into Janet's eyes.

'Well, shall we go and have our dinner?' said Nell.

'Another toast first,' said Janet.

They waited. Not even Nell knew what she was going to say. 'To Fidelia.'

'Don't spoil the party,' said Nell. 'But why the hell not? To Fidelia. Good fortune to Fidelia.'

'Who's she?' asked Bruce.

'The owner of this scarf,' said Nell.

'And of this necklace,' said Janet.

'Is she another of McAllister's guests?' asked Douglas. He put a sarcastic emphasis on the word.

'She's a very unfortunate woman,' said Janet.

214

15

The room looked out on to the hotel car park with only a glimpse of the sea-loch but the four sitting down to dinner were not concerned with scenery. There was a vase of roses on the table but they were hardly noticed. The food, which included Mary's special trifle, was appreciated but not discussed. Even the wine, the hotel's best, at ten pounds a bottle, was drunk without the praise it deserved. In spite of Nell's glowers, Janet set out to spoil the party. Before they were seated, she began to talk about Fidelia. She had on her witch's cap all right, though Nell, not having second sight, could not see it.

When she had finished her account, she sat pale-faced and trembling.

If ever there was a woman needing to be treated with caution, here she was. Bruce and Nell exchanged quick winks. Jephthah's daughter? asked Bruce's. Who else? replied Nell's.

Douglas, however, so delicate with his chip shots around the green, showed now the tact of a gorilla.

'That's all very well, Janet,' he said. 'You've just heard her side of the story. A father's got rights too, you know.'

He was lucky he didn't get a roast potato between his eyes.

'Of course, I'm sorry for the woman,' he went on. 'We're all sorry for her. But you've said yourself he's got the law on his side. Now, whether or not we think the law's an ass, we've got to respect it. It's the rule of law that upholds civilisation. Isn't that so?'

'I should have known your opinion would be crass.'

'What's crass about saying that the law's got to be respected? All right, if it's a bad law then change it, but do it constitutionally.

'We're talking about a woman who's having her kid taken from her.'

'It's the same principle, Nell. The law's decided against her.'

'What kind of law is it,' asked Janet, 'that says a child should be taken from her mother who's looked after her since she was born and given to a man who's never shown any interest in her before and who makes his living out of prostitution?'

'That's her version, Janet. Have you heard his?'

'Why has she never got a divorce?' asked Bruce. 'That way she could have kept her kid.'

'She's a Catholic,' said Nell. 'Very devout. Prays to the Sacred Heart. Doesn't believe in divorce. Her own worst enemy. We don't really know her. She's got the blood of savages in her. There's a funny look in her eyes every now and then.'

'But she needs help,' said Bruce. 'I'm not surprised she's not getting it from McAllister. I always thought he was a selfish bastard.'

'Angus just wants to paint,' said Nell. 'What's wrong with that?'

'It seems to me a very selfish attitude,' said Douglas. 'But isn't there someone you left out, Janet? The girl herself, this Letty. What does she want? Has anyone asked her?'

'She wants her father and mother to be together,' said Nell, 'as any child would.'

'Well, maybe that's what Gomez is here for.'

'It isn't,' said Janet.

'I expect if it was put to the child she'd have to say she wants to stay with her mother. That's natural. But what does she really want? We don't know that.'

'She told me twice that her father's rich,' said Nell. 'I bet she wouldn't mind living in Forbes Park.'

That had to be explained to Douglas. He said he wouldn't mind living there himself.

216

If, thought Nell, he came to Flodday hoping for a happy reconciliation in bed, he's going the wrong way about it. All the same, she couldn't help liking him for his – yes, crass was the word – crass but honest opinions.

He now uttered one of his crassest. 'Whatever the rights or wrongs of it, Janet, I don't think you should get mixed up in it. They're foreigners. Let them sort it out themselves. They've no right bringing their problems here.'

'What's Fidelia's nationality?' asked Bruce.

'She's Filipina,' said Janet, 'but she's lived many years in Basah.'

'Which is now part of Malaysia. Where was the kid born?'

'In Basah, I think.'

'Then she's a Malaysian. Gomez might have no claim on her. It would be worth investigating. She needs a better lawyer than Patel.'

'It would take a hell of a lot of money,' said Nell.

'If we all put together,' said Janet, 'we could do it.'

What they put together was their sense of shock and disbelief. It was in all their eyes as they stared at her.

'Angus too,' she added.

'If there was a chance of it coming off,' said Bruce, 'it might be worth trying, but there's no chance.'

Douglas could hardly speak for incredulity. 'Are you suggesting that we should finance this woman's lawsuit?'

'Yes, I am.'

'Do you know what lawsuits cost? There was a libel case reported in the *Herald* the other day that lasted only a week and cost a million pounds. A lawsuit's the quickest way to ruin yourself financially.'

'Wouldn't you take that risk to see justice done?'

'For a stranger? A foreigner? An Asiatic?'

It looked, thought Nell, as if Janet the witch was about to turn him into something loathsome, like a crocodile. But perhaps he was immune to her magic. In any case, he was already like a crocodile, in the thickness of his skin.

'I must say, Janet,' he grumbled, 'you've managed to spoil our celebration dinner.'

16

After dinner Nell and Bruce went to join in a ceilidh in the lounge bar. Later Douglas slunk in without Janet. Sad Gaelic songs were sung merrily, with everyone roaring out the choruses. A piper played a lament. Flodday Mist flowed. Emboldened by it, Douglas, the only man there, except the piper, wearing a kilt, volunteered to sing 'Sweet Rothesay Bay', which he'd often done at golf-club dos. His forebears, he explained, had come from Rothesay. In the old days it too had been a Gaelic town. He was vociferously applauded. He forgot Janet's unjust rejection of him.

The singing could be heard at the harbour where Janet had gone to throw bread to the swans. Though after ten, it was still daylight. She was thinking of the unhappy people at Ardnave, threatened by demons. She could do nothing to save them. She knew that something dreadful was going to happen but she did not know what and, even if she did, she could do nothing to prevent it. That was what had caused Aunt Chrissie to go mad. She had foreseen the deaths of friends in a boating accident. Similarly, at Ardnave, the tragedy, whatever it was, could not be averted.

Shortly after midnight the ceilidh broke up. Nell and Bruce went off to bed hand in hand and humming an air that had taken their fancy. He had consumed a quantity of wine, whisky, and beer, but was not, she hoped, drunk and incapable. He might in fact be sober enough to notice and be disgusted by the fat which she had let accumulate over the past two or three years and in which her jogging and her abstinence from alcohol had so far caused little decrease. When her bra was removed her breasts would sag, like loofahs: a sight that might inspire fond love in a cannibal chief but not in an Australian with recent experience of boobs like apples and pears. Worse still, when her girdle was removed, and it would be one hell of a job removing it, as it had been getting it on, her belly would overflow, like the bloody Nile, and she would stand revealed as a fat slob. Bruce, on the other hand, except for his paunch, was still a big handsome man whom any woman would be delighted to sleep with.

In their bedroom she asked him not to switch on the light: the moonlight was more romantic. He quickly stripped off until he was as naked as in the honeymoon photograph. As if remembering that occasion himself, he struck the same pose.

There was no time to lose. It would not do to keep any man, however virile, hanging about too long, especially if he had drunk a lot and might fall asleep at any moment. Unfortunately, the girdle proved as difficult as she had feared. No matter how she pushed, pulled, and wriggled, it would not go up over her breasts or down over her hips.

Below in the street some revellers were staggering home singing Gaelic hymns.

Bruce came to her assistance. To make it easier for him she lay down on the creaking bed and held her breath. He took a firm grip and tugged. The girdle tore. It came off then as easily as a banana skin and was tossed aside.

He crawled into bed beside her. It creaked mightily. They laughed. Joyfully they made love.

'I'm not past having a kid,' she murmured, and thought, fondly enough, of Angus.

'I'm not past it either.'

'Too true you aren't.'

'A girl, Nell, or a boy?'

220

'Why not twins? This is worth twins at least.'

'At least.'

It was then that Nell, as happy as she had ever been in her life, remembered poor Fidelia and wished her well.

In Room 18 Douglas was feeling seedy after so many mixed drinks. He was also feeling self-piteous. Not because Janet had sent word through David that she was sleeping in the brush cupboard that night. In his present state he couldn't have managed it with Elsie Hamilton, who helped more than she should, far less Janet demanding magic from him. No, the reason was that he had fallen into one of his fits of depression when he felt that he was not appreciated as he should be, as a golfer, as a singer, as a wearer of a kilt, as a civil engineer, and generally as a good fellow. They affected him only when he had had too much to drink and, of course, in the morning they were all gone. Tonight, in an effort to cheer himself up, he admired himself in the long mirror, first wearing his kilt and then only his jockstrap; soon he took that off too. Alas, his symbol of virility lay sulking like a puppy in disgrace and refused to perk up in spite of his coaxings. Nonetheless he was proud of it. It was his, and only his. He might let women like Cissie and Elsie have a loan of it as it were, for they could be depended on to let him have it back undamaged and recognisable. Not his Janet, though. He would never forget the night when she had come in and caught him looking at himself like this. Instead of pretending not to have seen, as a modest wife ought to, she had gone down on her knees and kissed him *there*. Never had he felt more embarrassed and less concupiscent. He had gone to bed in a huff, with his back to her, for a change.

In their room David and Mary were discussing Janet and Douglas. Janet had told David that she might not be returning to Clarkston with Douglas on Monday: she might never be going back there. Did she intend to stay at Ardnave with McAllister? asked Mary. No, though she was going to Ardnave tomorrow morning to find out what had happened between Mrs Gomez and her husband.

Before she fell asleep, Mary murmured that, if anyone ever tried to take her girls from her, she would kill him.

David lay awake a little while longer, wondering and shuddering.

17

As soon as the car with Janet, Nell, and the two girls drove off, Angus made for his studio, now a refuge rather than a place of work. Fidelia saw him sneak off but said nothing. Later he heard her go upstairs, no doubt to do some more praying. Only if they avoided each other could the hours between now and tomorrow at eleven be passed bearably. What he had said to Janet about putting his work first, no matter who got hurt, he had meant, though in his studio he just sat with his head down and stared at the floor. This crisis would pass. However it was solved, they would all have gone. He would then be able to raise his head again and get back to his painting.

What else could he do? Janet, apparently so devoted to Fidelia, had deserted her. He did not know what was going to happen tomorrow when Gomez came but, whatever it was, he was determined to have no part in it. He might not even remain in the house while the bargaining was going on. He had never had any authority, not of that kind anyway, and he was not prepared to claim any now. He was sure Fidelia would understand.

Letty did, as she soon showed. Instead of going upstairs with her mother, she hung about outside for a while and then came knocking at his door.

He was surprised as well as annoyed. He had heard Janet and Nell warning her not to disturb him while he was an his studio, and she had kept well away from him.

She kept on knocking. 'Mr McAllister,' she said, 'I want to talk to you.'

He could think of nothing that he could usefully say to her. 'I'm busy,' he called.

'No, you're not. I looked in the window. You're just sitting.'

'What do you want to talk to me about?'

'I'll tell you when you let me in.'

'Your mother needs you.'

'No, she doesn't. She's just praying.'

The scorn that she put into those words caused him, an agnostic, to shiver. She was too young to have dismissed God.

He got up and opened the door.

She went in. Though she wasn't there as an art critic, she stared for a minute or so at 'Taurus'. Is that supposed to be a painting?' she asked.

'It will be when it's finished.'

'I think it's stupid. Was it you who painted the birds and butterflies on the stairs?'

'Yes.'

'They're nice. I like them. I don't like *this*, and I don't like the picture of my mother in your room. Why do like painting ladies with no clothes on?'

He could find no ready answer.

She wasn't going to argue about it. These were preliminary palavers.

'Can I sit down, please?'

'If you can find a seat.'

She upturned a wastepaper bucket and sat on it. 'You sit down too.'

He sat down.

'I don't like you,' she said.

He did not have to ask why. He knew. He had made use of her mother and now was abandoning her. The child was justified in not liking him.

'I'm sorry.'

'No, you're not. You don't care if I like you or not.'

224

Was that true? If it was, it meant that he was even more callous than he had thought. But yes, it *was* true. He did not care whether anyone liked him or not. It was an admission that would haunt him till the day he died but it had to be made.

'Do you like my mother?' she asked.

Who had put her up to asking these questions? If Janet had been there, he would have blamed her. He could never have blamed Fidelia. She had always sought to build up his self-esteem, never to destroy it.

Letty was finding the questions herself. She was still waiting for an answer.

'Yes, I like your mother.'

She did not ask, as Janet and Nell would have done, why, if he liked Fidelia, he was doing nothing to help her. Nor did she accuse him of lying. She seemed to accept that he did like her mother, but it didn't matter, his liking of her mother wasn't important.

'My father's coming here tomorrow, isn't he?'

'Yes.'

'I'm glad.'

'Have you ever met your father?'

'No, but I've seen him, in a photograph.'

He wasn't surprised to hear that Fidelia had kept a photograph of her husband. Perhaps it had been added to the saints on her shrine.

'My father's got lots of money.'

Who had told her? Her mother? Also impressed by Gomez's wealth? It was possible.

'He's coming to take me away.'

Had her mother told her that too? What else? That if she wanted to go with her father, her mother would not try to stop her? Fidelia the martyr.

He should have kept out of it. 'Do you want to go with him?' he asked.

225

After a long pause she replied: 'If my mother can come too.'

Was that Fidelia's hope? That Gomez would want them both? Was that what she was praying for? Well, she would make a good submissive wife. Was their story going to have a happy ending after all? He hoped so. He would claim no credit but he would share in the general relief. Could he, he wondered, interest Gomez in buying the portrait of Fidelia? It was his masterpiece so far but if he got rid of her in person it might be as well to get rid of her also as a painting.

Letty, he saw, had none of her mother's primitive reverence. Though brought up a Catholic, she already had more faith in money than in prayer as a producer of miracles. In Basah it had been part of Fidelia's charm. Here it was more like a mental retardation. She could never be happy in this temperate, thin-lipped, pink-skinned, sceptical country. It would have been cruelty to try to keep her here.

When he went up to bed he locked his door. It was the first time he had ever done so. He had had to search for the key.

He had been in bed for half an hour or so when he remembered he had forgotten to put out bread for the demons. As he lay wondering whether he should get up and do it, he became aware that there was someone in the lobby and then his door handle turned. It could only be Fidelia. She had waited till Letty was asleep. But what did she want? What did she have to say to him or offer him that would make any difference? Although she was silent, hardly breathing, he could tell that she was waiting outside the door. Perhaps she was considering whether to call his name and beg him to let her in. If she did, he would go on pretending to be asleep. He thought he heard her softly weeping, but it could have been his imagination.

At last she went away. He heard the floorboards creaking. Wondering as to what her purpose could have been, he forgot the bread for the demons.

18

Next morning Fidelia appeared in the living-room dressed in sarong and *kebaya*, red with black dragon designs, surely pagan in origin. She had a gold crucifix round her neck. Was this display of Oriental beauty and Catholic piety intended to impress Gomez?

Leaving her to make breakfast for herself and Letty, he went out to walk on the beach, with Janet's imaginary monks. It was a glorious morning. Never had Ardnave, indeed all of Flodday, looked more heavenly. Since it was Sunday, there might be an invasion of tourists and natives, undeterred by the notices Beware of the Bull, which he had persuaded Mr McCandlish to put up.

He had on his green corduroy suit and a clean white shirt. Whatever other role he ought to be playing, he was at any rate the host. Earlier, when washing, he had seen how thinner and more austere his face had grown during the past week.

He had still to decide what he should do when the visitors came. He could approach them courteously, saying that Mrs Gomez and her daughter were in the house waiting, and then he could go for a meditative walk on the machair. Or he could accompany the visitors into the house. In the latter case, what attitude should he adopt? He had no right to interfere between a husband and wife. Were even the police not reluctant to do so? Perhaps he could best help by sitting in wise silence, like another Buddha.

He saw Letty making faces at him out of an upstairs window. He moved behind the rocks that Janet had mistaken for monks.

He heard the car before he saw it. Black as a hearse, it came slowly along the track towards the house. Were its occupants admiring the scenery?

He went up the path past the monks' privy and approached the car, which had stopped outside the house. The chauffeur got out and opened the door. Gomez was first to emerge. He was wearing a white suit with red-toed shoes. He took off his hat and revealed black hair glistening with sweet oil. Immediately flies came from cowpats to besiege him. Peevishly he tried to drive them off with his hat. Here he had no hired thugs to protect him.

The lawyer was older and more soberly dressed. He was carrying a briefcase.

Gomez caught sight of Angus's shrine. He was not sure of its significance. Did he take it to be Catholic, with the Virgin and Child missing? With his left hand he vaguely crossed himself.

Angus did not offer to shake hands. His posture must be one of serene impartiality.

'Señor Gomez?' he asked.

'Yes.'

Gomez's eyes, like Fidelia's, like all Asia's, were brown, but his were also sly and knowing. What they knew was the price of everything. Love could be bought as easily as gold tiepins by someone with as much money as he.

Still, if Angus was to be true to his role of Buddha's understudy, he had to be unprejudiced and fair. In Manila Gomez was probably a man of substance and respectability, friendly with bishops and politicians.

His eyes appraised Angus: they had already appraised the house. Angus saw himself dismissed as an obscure painter of no consequence, living in a wilderness with heaps of cow shit almost on his doorstep.

He noticed then the resemblance between Gomez and Letty.

The lawyer's eyes were blank. His business was with documents. 'You will know, Mr McAllister, that we have come to discuss certain matters with Miss Diaz. Is she in the house?'

Angus knew that Fidelia's maiden name was Diaz. Why was this fellow referring to her by it? Was it some Filipino trick?

'Mrs Gomez is in the house,' he said, 'and her daughter.'

Both Gomez and the lawyer looked relieved. They must have feared that Fidelia and Letty had been smuggled away.

'Our business is with them,' said the lawyer, 'but we do not object if you are present. We agree that you are to a certain extent involved.'

Do you really? cried Angus, inwardly. Well, let me tell you, I do not consider myself involved in any way.

That was cowardly. Being brave would have had him scaring off these vultures. But bravery not infrequently was rash. Fidelia did not want them to be scared off. In her present self-sacrificial and penitential mood she had wanted them to come and, figuratively speaking, peck out her eyes and tear her living flesh to pieces. If that was what she and her God had decided between them, what right had he to interfere?

'Please go in, gentlemen,' he said.

When Gomez saw the Balinese mask, he pretended to be amused but he was really terrified. It was how the fiends of hell were portrayed in Fidelia's book.

Fidelia and Letty were seated together on the green divan. Fidelia looked up at Gomez with a curious remote expression. He ignored her but smiled at Letty.

'Please sit down,' said Angus.

Gomez sat on the yellow divan, with his hat on his knees. The lawyer murmured that, if Mr McAllister did not mind, he would stand.

Angus himself sat on the red divan.

The lawyer stood close to Buddha. He had taken some documents out of his briefcase.

Letty couldn't keep her eyes off her father. She seemed to be fascinated by his display of wealth: the expensive clothes, the three gold rings, and the gold tiepin with the diamond sparkling in it.

'I have here,' said the lawyer, 'copies of warrants issued by courts in the Philippines and Malaysia awarding custody of the child Letitia Gomez to her father Señor Enrique Gomez of Forbes Park, Manila.' He offered to show them to Angus, but not to Fidelia.

Angus declined. 'Are they enforceable in Scotland?' he asked, neutrally.

'Ultimately, yes, Mr McAllister. No country will give coun-tenance to a lawbreaker. By disregarding these warrants and abducting the child, Miss Diaz has broken the laws of two countries, as she well knows. She has acted contrary to the advice of her lawyer, Mr Patel.'

Inwardly Angus retorted: 'No fair-minded person in this or any other country would consider Miss Diaz, as you call her, a lawbreaker. For ten years she has looked after her child while Mr Gomez showed no interest. Morally, therefore, if not legally, he has forfeited any right he may have had to the child.'

Outwardly he said nothing. He was leaving it to Fidelia. Unlike him she was running a great risk in not speaking up. Was it possible that she had let Letty coax or bully her into surrender, in return perhaps for monetary compensation?

The lawyer was holding up another document. 'Some time ago, in Manila, a decree of annulment of marriage was granted to Señor Gomez by the appropriate authorities.'

By his friends the bishops! Angus could not keep indignation out of his voice. 'How could she be divorced without her knowledge?'

'It has been done. May I point out that there is now no impediment to your marriage with Miss Diaz, which we under-stand has been your wish for some time.'

Angus ought not to have shaken his head or looked dismayed, but he did. He saw Fidelia gazing at him and tried to smile.

230

'This being so,' said the lawyer, 'it is in the child's best interests that she be taken into the care of her natural and legal father.'

This time Angus nodded, without meaning to, without knowing what it was supposed to convey.

Fidelia then, up to that moment passive and meek as a nun in prayer, giving the impression that she was prepared to bear without complaint whatever cross God laid upon her, suddenly sprang to her feet, with a bound reached the blowpipe-spear, tore it down off the wall, gripped it fiercely in both hands, with the spear part foremost, and rushed to plunge it into Gomez's breast as Angus thought and Gomez too, judging by his look of terror, but no, to Angus's incredulity and shock, it was into Angus's own breast that the sharp iron point was plunged with force enough to embed it deeply, with blood bursting out and covering his white shirt in an instant. Thus had headhunters finished off the wild pigs which their poisoned darts had first paralysed. He could not think clearly: the pain was too great. He heard screaming: it was little Letty's. Did it have in it a trace of jubilation? He should not have forgotten to put out bread for the demons. Fidelia was staring down at him, her face contorted with horror: no wonder, considering what a hideous mistake she had made. But why wasn't she wiping the blood from his mouth? He heard a car stopping outside. It must be Janet, come too late. The funny thing was he felt animosity towards no one.